THE LAST PRINCE
OF DAHAAR

BY
TARA PAMMI

Published in Great Britain 2014
by Mills & Boon, an imprint of Harlequin (UK) Limited,
Eton House, 18-24 Paradise Road, Richmond, Surrey, TW9 1SR

© 2014 Tara Pammi

ISBN: 978 0 263 90847 3

Harlequin (UK) Limited's policy is to use papers that are natural,
renewable and recyclable products and made from wood grown in
sustainable forests. The logging and manufacturing processes conform
to the legal environmental regulations of the country of origin.

Printed and bound in Spain
by Blackprint CPI, Barcelona

Tara Pammi can't remember a moment when she wasn't lost in a book—especially a Mills & Boon® romance, which provided so much more excitement to a teenager than a mathematics textbook. It was only years later, while struggling with her two-hundred-page thesis in a basement lab, that Tara realised what she really wanted to do: write a romance novel. She already had the requirements—a wild imagination and a love for the written word.

Tara lives in Colorado with the most co-operative man on the planet and two daughters. Her husband and daughters are the only things that stand between Tara and a full-blown hermit life with only books for company.

Tara would love to hear from readers. She can be reached at tara.pammi@gmail.com or through her website: www.tarapammi.com

Recent titles by the same author:

A TOUCH OF TEMPTATION*
A HINT OF SCANDAL*

The Sensational Stanton sisters

For my brother—
I'm so proud of the man you have become.

With such real-life inspiration, no wonder the hero
of this book is such an awesome son and brother.

CHAPTER ONE

PUMP HIS BODY full of narcotics and fall into blessed oblivion? Or suffer a fitful sleep and welcome the madness within to take over?

Abuse his body or torture his mind?

It was a choice Ayaan bin Riyaaz Al-Sharif, the crown prince of Dahaar, faced every evening when dusk gave way to dark night.

After eight months of lucidity, and he used the term very loosely, he had no idea which he would favor on a given day.

Tonight, he was leaning toward the drugs.

It was his last night as a guest in Siyaad, the neighboring nation to his own country, Dahaar. He would be better off knocking himself out.

You did that last night too, a voice whispered in his ear. A voice that sounded very much like his older brother, who had spent countless hours toughening up Ayaan.

Stepping out of the blisteringly hot shower, Ayaan dried himself and pulled on black sweatpants. He had run for three hours straight tonight, setting himself a pace that lit a fire in his muscles. His body felt like a mass of bruised pulp.

He had kept to lighted grounds, to the perimeter of the palace. And every time he'd spotted a member of the royal guard—both his own and Siyaadi—his breath had come a little more easily.

Walking back into the huge bedroom, he eyed the bottle of narcotics on his bedside table. Two tablets and he would be out like the dead.

The option was infinitely tempting. So what if he felt lousy tomorrow with a woozy head and woolen mouth?

Another night would pass without incident, without an *episode*. Another night where he accepted defeat, accepted his powerlessness in his fight against his own mind.

Defeat...

He picked up the plastic bottle and turned it around, playing with the cap, almost tasting the bitter pill on his tongue.

A breeze flew in through the French doors, blowing the sheer silk curtains up. Dark had fallen in the past half hour, the heat of the evening touched by its cold finger.

Peaceful, quiet nights were not his friends. Peaceful, quiet nights *in a strange place* were enough to bring him to his knees, reducing him to a mindless, useless coward.

He was still a bloody coward, afraid of his own shadow.

Powerless fury roared through him, and he threw the painkillers across the empty room. The bottle hit the wall with a soft thud and disappeared beneath an antique armoire.

A quiet hush followed the sound of the bottle, the silence beginning to settle over his skin like a chilly blanket.

He grabbed the remote and turned on the huge plasma TV on the opposite wall. He had specifically requested the guest suite with the largest TV. Flipping to a soccer game, he turned the volume up so high that the sounds reverberated around him. Soon, his skull would hurt at the pounding din of it, the echoes ringing in his ears. But he welcomed the physical discomfort, even though at this rate, he would be deaf by the time he was thirty.

Walking around the room, he turned off the lights.

As his eyes became accustomed to the dark, he got into bed. A pulse of distress traveled up his spine and knotted up at the base of his neck. He curled his fists, focusing on the simple act of breathing in and out. He willed his mind to understand, to stop looping back at its own fears and feeding on them.

Sleep came upon him hard, a deceptive haven capable of snatching control from him and reducing him into a cowering animal.

Zohra Katherine Naasar Al-Akhtum slowly made her way through the lighted corridors toward the guest suite that was situated in the wing farthest from the main residence wings of the palace.

Her feet, clad in leather slippers, didn't make a sound on the pristine marble floors. But her heart thumped in her chest, and with each step, her feet dragged on the floor.

It was half past eleven. She shouldn't be out of bed, much less roaming around in this part of the palace where women were expressly forbidden. Not that she had ever heeded the rules of the palace. She just hadn't needed to be in here until now.

Now…now she had no choice.

She straightened her flagging spine and forged on.

The fact that she hadn't encountered a guard until now weighed heavily in her gut instead of easing her anxiety. It had been easy to bribe one of the maids and inquire which suite their esteemed guest was staying in.

Suddenly there she was, standing in front of centuries-old, intricately carved, gigantic oak doors. Zohra felt as if cold fingers had clamped over her spine.

Behind those doors was the man in whose hands her fate, her entire life, would lay if she didn't do something about it. And she couldn't accept that. If she had to give offense for it, take the most twisted way out of it, so be it.

Sucking a deep breath, she pushed the doors and stepped in. The main lounge was quiet, the moonlight from the balcony on the right bathing it in a silvery glow. But the bedroom in the back, the sounds of a...soccer game boomed out of it.

Was the prince having a party while she was getting cold sweats just thinking about her future?

Straightening her shoulders, Zohra set off toward the bedroom. Flashes of light came and went, the sounds so loud that she couldn't distinguish one from the other.

She neared the wide entrance, crossed the threshold and came to a halt, her gaze drawn to the huge plasma screen on the opposite wall. It took her a moment to see through the flashes of light, to realize that there was no crowd in the room.

Scrunching her face against the loud noise from the speakers plugged in overhead and around the room, she searched for the remote. It was enough to give a person a pounding headache in minutes.

Flinching every time another roar went up, she walked around and found the remote on the bedside table. She quickly muted the television, the light from the bright screen casting enough glow to let her see the outline of the room.

With silence came another sound she hadn't heard until now. A sound that turned her skin clammy. The hairs on her arms stood up. It began again. A low, muffled cry, tempered by the sheets. Like a scream of utter pain, but locked away in someone's throat. She shivered, the agony in that sound crawling up her skin and latching on to the warmth.

Every instinct she possessed warned her to turn around and leave. She half turned on the balls of her feet, her neck cricking at the speed of it.

But the next sound that came from the bed was pure suffering. This time, it wasn't locked away. Neither was it loud but more gut-wrenching for the accompanying whimper it held.

The sound ripped through her, breathing the anguish of an unbearable pain into the very air around her.

She wanted to curl up, brace herself against it. Or at least run far from it.

And yet the agony in that cry…she would never forget it in this lifetime.

Zohra turned around and reached the bed. She almost tripped on the heavy stool that lay at the side of the bed in her hurry. Clutching the silk sheets with her fingers, she hefted herself onto the high bed.

Her blood running cold in her veins, she pushed through the sea of crumpled sheets, until her gaze fell on the man.

For a moment, she could do nothing but study him. His eyes were closed, his forehead bunched into a tight knot and his hands fisted on the sheets with a white-knuckled grip.

White lines fanned around his mouth, a lone tear escaping from his scrunched eyes. His forehead was bathed in sweat, as he thrashed against the sheets.

Pushing the sheets away, Zohra reached for his hands and gasped. He was ice-cold to the touch. Another soft whimper fell from his mouth.

A wave of powerlessness hit her. Shoving it away, she grabbed his shoulders, even knowing that trying to move him would be truly impossible. With strength that surprised even her, she tucked her hands under his rock-hard shoulders when his muscled arm shot out.

That arm hit her jaw with a force that rattled her teeth. She half slipped, half tumbled to the edge of the bed. Darts of pain radiated up her jaw. She swallowed the lump in her throat and pushed herself back onto the bed.

This time, she was prepared for him. She moved to the head of the bed, avoiding his arms and placing her hands either side of his face. A groan escaped his mouth again, and his fingers clamped over her wrists.

His grip was so tight but she ignored it and shook him hard. And then tapped his cheek, determined to break the choking grip of whatever stifled him.

She couldn't bear to hear that tortured sound anymore, not if there was any way she could wake him up.

"Wake up, *ya habibi*," she whispered, much like she had done with her brother Wasim when her stepmother had died six years ago. "It's just a nightmare." She ran her hands over his bare shoulders, over the high planes of his cheeks. She kept whispering the same words, much to her own benefit as his, as he continued to turn his head left and right.

"You need to wake up," she whispered again.

Suddenly his thrashing body stilled. His gaze flew open, and Zohra was looking into the most beautiful golden bronze gaze she had ever seen.

Her heart kicked against her ribs. With his hands still gripping her, she stared at him as he did her.

He had the most beautiful eyes—golden pupils with specks of copper and bronze, with lashes that curled toward angular cheekbones. But it wasn't the arresting colors of his gaze that made her chest tighten, that made it a chore to pull air in.

It was the unhidden pain that haunted those depths. His fingers caressed her wrists, as though to make sure she was there.

He closed his eyes, his breathing going from harsh to a softer rhythm and opened his eyes again.

It was as though she was looking into a different man's eyes.

His gaze was cautious at first, openly curious, next sweeping over her eyes, nose, lingering on her mouth, until a shadow cycled it to sheer fury.

It lit his gaze up like the blazing fire of a thousand suns.

He released her, pushed her back and she fell against the headboard with a soft gasp. He pulled himself up to his knees, his movements in no way reminiscent of the nightmare he had been fighting just moments ago. "Who are you?"

His words sounded rough, gravelly, which meant he had been screaming for a while before she had arrived.

Her chest tightened. "Are you okay?" she whispered, taking in the sheen of sweat on his forehead, the infinitesimal tremble in the set of his lean shoulders.

"How is that any of your business?" he roared. "I dismissed the guards hours ago. I was informed no one would be allowed into this wing per my orders. So what the hell are you doing here?"

That's why no one had stopped her. And he had the volume on the TV set to that earsplitting level as if he had known…

Zohra frowned. "I saw you thrashing on the sheets. I had to help."

"I could have hurt you."

She instantly tugged the sleeves of her tunic over her wrists.

His face could have been poured from concrete for the tightness that crept into it. Only the slight flare of his nostrils and the incandescent rage in his gaze said he was still a man and not one of the concrete busts of long-gone emperors and warriors scattered around the palace. "Turn on the lamp."

She leaned over and turned it on, her entire body feeling strangely awkward. The lamp was on her side and cast just enough glow to illuminate his face.

Ayaan bin Riyaaz Al-Sharif, the new crown prince of Dahaar was not what she had been expecting. The *Mad Prince*, that's what she had heard the Siyaadi palace staff whisper about him. Yet there was nothing remotely mad about the man staring at her with incisive intelligence in his eyes.

There had been only a single picture of him, a grainy one, eight months ago when Dahaar had jubilantly celebrated his return. He had been pronounced dead five years ago along with his older brother and sister—victims of a brutal terrorist attack.

But nothing more about him had been revealed, nor had he appeared anywhere in public. Even the ceremony where he had been declared crown prince had been private, which had only fueled the media and the public's hunger for information about him.

He had remained a shapeless, mindless figure at the back of her mind.

Until she had visited her father this afternoon. Weakened by a heart attack, the king had sounded feeble and yet his words had rung with pride and joy.

Prince Ayaan has agreed to marry you, Zohra. You will be the queen of Dahaar one day.

Suddenly, the Mad Prince had become the man who could bind her forever to the very world that had taken everything from her.

The reminder, however, did nothing to stem the quiet, relentless assault his very presence wreaked on her. She could no more stop her gaze from drifting over him than she could stop breathing.

He had a gaunt, chiseled look that added to the rumors swirling about him.

His face was long with a severe nose, a pointed chin, with cheekbones that were sharp enough to cut. His wavy, black hair curled onto his high forehead in an unkempt way. As if he had threaded his fingers through it and tugged at it viciously. The moment the thought crossed her mind, she knew it was true.

The tendons in his neck stood out. He was lean, bordering on thin and yet what flesh there was to him looked as if it had been carved out of rock.

A pale, inch-wide scar stretched from his left shoulder all the way to his ribs on the right side and beyond to his back. What could wield such a painful-looking scar?

Her empty stomach rolled on itself. How could a man withstand so much without...*going mad*?

The thought swept through her like a fierce cold wave, and she shivered.

His scrutiny as intent as her own, he said, "Hold out your hands," in a tone that held raw command.

Zohra sucked in a breath and tucked her hands behind her.

He moved on the bed with lithe grace that would have been beautiful to savor if her heart hadn't crawled into her throat. She was taller than the average Dahaaran woman and yet he towered over her.

The scent of him had a tang to it that made her suck in a quick, greedy breath even before she knew it. He tugged her hands forward in a sudden move.

Her skin stung where he had gripped her at even the slight friction of his fingers. He sucked in a deep breath.

As though he was bracing himself. His fingers gentled as he pushed the sleeves of her tunic back.

Dark impressions framed each wrist. A chill surrounded them, and she had the strangest feeling that his emotions were at the center of it.

She tugged at her hands but he didn't let go. "How long were you here before I woke up?"

The tension emanating from him rendered her mute.

"*How long?*"

He didn't shout the words yet they radiated with utter fury. "Five, maybe six minutes. I didn't know what to do."

He let go of her hands with a jerk. "You were not supposed to be in here in the first place. And if you're reckless enough to be, the minute you saw me, you should have turned around and walked out."

She shook her head. "I would loathe myself if I just walked away."

He ran a hand through his hair again, his movements visibly shaken. But he didn't get off the bed, blocking her escape. "It is a quarter to midnight. I have asked you twice why you are here. If you will not answer me, I will summon the guard. Before you realize it, you will be out of a job, out of a livelihood. All for what? To get a little information on the Mad Prince? A quick photograph, is that it? Tell me who sent you here and I will show lenience."

He thought she was a servant paid to gather information about him? "No one sent me here, Prince Ayaan."

He became stiffer, if possible, the rigid line of his shoulders obvious in the feeble light. The bones at the crook between his neck and shoulders stood out in stark relief.

She didn't want to antagonize him any more than she already had. She didn't want to ponder about his nightmare, his reaction to her being a witness to it. If she did this right, she wouldn't need to see him ever again nor hear the gut-wrenching pain she had heard in his cries.

"I...came here of my own volition. It was important for me to talk to you before you left tomorrow morning."

Slowly, the annoyance in his expression shifted to watchfulness. And she fought the need to shy away from it, to hide from his intense scrutiny.

He knew.

She could pinpoint the exact moment he realized—the watchfulness turned into realization, a flare of color in those beautiful eyes.

That gaze moved over her in a slow sweep, lingering over her face for the longest time, seeing her with new eyes. This time, it wasn't mere anger that colored it, but wariness, almost as if she had suddenly become dangerous to him.

"Of course you're not a servant."

He stepped off the bed as though he couldn't breathe the same air for another moment. She stared at the broad expanse of his back. The scar streaked through his back too, like a rope bound around his body.

He pulled on a T-shirt and stood by the foot of the enormous bed, his hands behind him, as though waiting for her to come to her senses.

Heat spread up her neck and she gritted her teeth.

She had nothing to feel guilty or ashamed about. She had seized the only opportunity available to her. She had seen a man in the throes of a violent nightmare and tried to help.

She slid to her feet, the muscles in her legs trembling.

"What was so important that it had to be said in the middle of the night?"

This was it. This was why she had risked coming into

his suite. And yet, her tongue felt as if it was glued to the roof of her mouth.

"Should I send word to King Salim?"

She stared at him, the sudden threat in his words, the raw command showing a different man. "There's no need to involve my father in a matter that concerns me…*us*. I'm sure we can settle this between ourselves and come to a conclusion that is agreeable to both of us."

CHAPTER TWO

SHE WAS HIS *betrothed*.

Ayaan felt the world tilting at his feet as what he had guessed curdled into undeniable reality.

This slip of a woman, who had the nerve to climb onto his bed and hold him through a nightmare, this woman, who was even now meeting his gaze with an arrogant confidence, was the woman he had agreed to marry just a few hours ago?

He hadn't given her a moment's thought. She was nothing more than a bullet point in the list of things he had agreed to in the name of duty.

He stood unmoving, the need to vent his spiraling frustration burning his muscles.

Her light brown hair was combed away into a braid. Her eyes were brown, huge in her long face. A strong nose and mouth followed, the stubborn jut of it saying so much about the woman.

She wore a light pink tunic over black leggings, a flimsy shawl wrapped loosely around her torso. Her outfit was plain for a princess, giving no hint as to what lay…

With a control he had honed tight over the past few months, he brought his gaze back to her face. He had indulged himself enough. How the woman looked, or what kind of a body she had, held no significance to him.

Her mother had been American, someone had mentioned it to him. But she was a copy of King Salim. The same no-nonsense air about her, the proud chin, the dogged determination it must have cost her to be near him during his nightmare.

He had no doubt about how violent he could get when caught in one of those nocturnal episodes. It was the reason he detested having anyone even within hearing distance. And despite every precaution he took to hide the truth, to spare his parents, they had already earned him the title of Mad Prince.

If only the world knew what a luxury madness was compared to his lucidity.

He didn't want to marry this woman any more than he wanted the mantle of Dahaar. The latter, he had been able to postpone. The former…?

The people of Dahaar need reassurance that all is well with you, they need a reason to celebrate. They haven't had one in five years. And Siyaad needs our help. King Salim stood by me when I had no one else to rely on, when I was crumbling under the weight of Dahaar.

Now it is time we return the favor.

Ayaan wasn't prepared for it. He would never be.

How could he be, when he didn't trust himself, when he didn't know what could break him again, when he was constantly hovering over the thin line between lucidity and lunacy?

But he couldn't refuse his father, not after everything he had gone through to rule and protect Dahaar, after losing his eldest son and daughter, losing Ayaan to insanity.

His parents had lost everything in one night, but they hadn't broken. They hadn't failed in their duty. He couldn't either.

But suddenly, King Salim's profuse excuses at tonight's

dinner made sense. His daughter's absence had been an act of defiance. Not that Ayaan had cared that she was absent. On the contrary, he had been glad that he didn't need to give the concept of his betrothed a concrete form until that moment was absolutely upon him.

And now here she was, pushing herself into his mind in a way he couldn't just undo. Within five minutes spent in her company, he already knew more about her than he wanted to learn in a lifetime. She was stubborn, she was brave and the worst? She wasn't conventional.

"I understood you were too ill to be out and about, Princess Zohra," he said, forcing utter scorn into his words. "And yet here you are, walking around the palace at night, disrupting a guest's privacy, offering insult."

"Do not call me a princess. I have never been one."

He was too...*irritated* to even ask her why.

He was chilled to the bone, as he always was when he woke up from one of his nightmares. "Fine. Please tell me why you are in my bed, in my suite, in the palace wing that is strictly forbidden to women, at the stroke of midnight. What was so important that you had to—"

"You were thrashing in the bed, crying out. I couldn't just stand by and do nothing. Nor could I walk away and come back at a better time."

"Are you deaf? Or just plain dense?" The words roared out of him on a wave of utter shame. He gritted his teeth, fighting for control over a temper that never flared. "Why are you here in the first place?"

The brown of her eyes expanded, her mouth dropping open on a soft huff. His uncivilized words chased away the one thing he couldn't bear to see—her pity.

"If you think you can scare me into running away by behaving like a savage, it won't work."

He could have laughed if he wasn't so wound up. Every

inch of her—her head held high, the deprecation in her look, the stubborn jut of her chin—she was a princess no matter what she said. "If this were Dahaar, I would have—"

"But it's not Dahaar. Nor am I your loyal subject dependent on your tender mercies," she said, steel creeping into her words. "This is Siyaad. And even here, all those rules, they don't apply to me." Her eyes collided with his, daring him to challenge her claim. When Ayaan said nothing, her gaze swept over his features with a thoroughness that she couldn't hide. Did she feel the same burn of awareness that arched into life suddenly? "I came to inform you that it's not worth it."

Ayaan had known only one woman in his life who had had the temerity and the confidence to speak to him like that—Amira, his older sister. A sliver of pain sliced through his gut. Amira had never let Azeez or him get by with anything. And it had been more because of her core of steel than because she had been born into an extremely powerful family.

He had a feeling the same was true of the woman who met his gaze unflinchingly.

"What is not worth it?"

"Marrying me."

"Why are you telling me this instead of your father?"

She blinked but it didn't hide the pain that filled her eyes. "I… He is not well. I could not…take the chance and risk making him worse."

"Being here with me, persuading me why you are not *worth it* does not harm him?"

A shrug of those slender shoulders. "If you refuse me, he would be disappointed, yes. But not surprised."

He frowned at her conclusion. "So you want me to do your dirty work for you?"

She took a deep breath and his curiosity mounted. "I'm not shy, willing, happy to be a man's shadow—the kind of woman whose only mission in life would be to spew out your heirs every other year. I have never been and it's not a role one grows into."

Ayaan smiled, despite the irritation flickering through him.

The woman had gall. And even without her mission statement just now, it was clear she wasn't a woman who could tolerate the traditional marriage their countries dictated.

Then why was King Salim pushing for this marriage? He had to know that Ayaan and his father would stand beside him without this marriage clause, and yet he had shown more enthusiasm for it.

"If you had attended the dinner and did your duty, I could have told you what I want in my wife."

She shook her head, her breath quickening. "What is there to learn? The wives—they are nothing but bloodlines and broodmares. Even a harem girl probably has it better than the dutiful wife of the king. At least, she gets good sex out of the…"

He burst out laughing. His chest heaved with it, the sound barreling out of him. Even his throat felt raw in a strange way.

He couldn't help taking a step toward her.

Pink stole into her cheeks, and she looked away from him, something unintelligible falling from her mouth.

Her long lashes cast shadows onto sharply fragile cheekbones, her mouth—unpainted and pink. The slow burn under his skin gathered momentum. He had never liked the scent of roses growing up, it had pervaded the palace, his own chamber and sometimes, even his clothes. Yet the scent of her skin danced beneath it, teasing, tempting, coated with her awareness of him.

"So you would prefer to be part of my harem instead of my wife?"

Her gaze widened, her mouth opening and closing. "This is my life we're talking about."

He came to a stop near her and leaned against the bed, enjoying the proximity of her presence. It didn't fill him with the suffocating tension that everyone else's did since his return. "You haven't said a single word that would make me take you seriously, Princess." She opened her mouth but he didn't give her the chance. "All I see is a woman throwing a tantrum like a petulant teenager instead of doing her duty. What if someone had seen you come into my suite? You risk exposing yourself to ridicule and scandal, adding to your father's burden."

She didn't like that. He could see it in her eyes. "Of course, you wouldn't want someone petulant like me to be the future queen of Dahaar, would you?"

"So, this is all to prove a point?"

"I don't have any duty toward Siyaad. And nothing will make me feel anything more for Dahaar either." She took a deep breath, as though bracing herself. "Marrying me will only bring shame to you and the royal house of Dahaar."

He covered the distance between them, knowing that she was baiting him yet unable to resist. "Why does that sound more like a threat and less like a warning?" he whispered.

"I'm simply telling you the truth. Whatever expectations you have of your bride, I will fail them."

Ayaan frowned, regretting not learning more about her before he had given his word. "If this is about *your* expectations of this marriage, state them."

Zohra tamped down the scream building inside her chest looking for an outlet. He wasn't supposed to ask her what she wanted out of this marriage. He was supposed to sputter in outrage, call her disobedient, scandalous…

Any other man in his place would have called her behavior an insult. He would have gone straight to her father and broken the alliance.

"The only expectation I have of you," she said, feeling as though she was stepping over an unknown threshold, "is that you use the power you have to refuse this marriage."

A neat little frown appeared between his brows. "Unless I have a strong reason for it, it would be termed as an insult to your father, to you and to Siyaad."

"Isn't it enough that you have zero interest in marrying me?"

"I have zero interest in marrying anyone. But I will do it for—"

"For your country, yes, I know that," she spat the words out, feeling that sense of isolation that had been her constant companion for eleven years. She had never belonged in Siyaad, never felt as if she was a part of it. "But I'm not duty bound as you are. All I want is the freedom to live my life away from the shackles of this kind. And if it is a crystal clear reason that you want, then I will give you one."

"You have my full attention, Princess." There was a dangerous inflection in his voice where it had been void of anything else before.

She wet her lips, praying her voice would hold steady when she was shaking inside. "I'm not future queen material. I don't give a fig about duty and all that it entails. I'm educated *and* I'm smart enough to have my own opinions, which, I have been informed, are enough to drive a man up the wall. I'm a…*bastard*." She had to breathe through the lump growing in her throat. "My father lived with my mother until I was seven but he…never married her. He became my guardian when she died."

Not even by the flicker of an eyelid did he betray his reaction. "Is that all?"

Curse the man to hell and back. Desperation tied her insides into painful knots. "No, there's one last reason— the most important of all."

"Don't stop now," he said, his voice laced with mockery.

"I'm not a chaste virgin with an unblemished reputation." Her chest was so tight she wondered if she was getting any air. "I would rather you refuse me now than claim that you've been cheated when you...find out."

He ran his forefinger over his temple, his expression betraying nothing. Her heartbeat ratcheted up. "When I find out that you're not a virgin?"

Fierce heat blanketed her, even as shock stung her. Why wasn't the man throwing a royal fit even now? "When you find out that I was in love with another man, when you find out that I have spent four summers with him in a desert encampment..." She swallowed painfully, just the thought of Faisal slashing pain through her.

"That is...a valid reason for me to refuse you," he finally said.

Zohra felt the most perverse disappointment. He had been unlike anything she had imagined until now.

"So are you prepared for your father's reaction when I present him with this...reason?"

Her gut dropped to her feet. "What do you mean?"

"I told you. I have no wish to insult your father after everything he has done to stand by mine. You might not feel any duty to your country. But are you so selfish that you would put your father through this? He will not only be shamed by his daughter's behavior but he will be so in front of an audience."

She flinched at the distaste in his words. He hadn't intended to back out for a second. Her gut churned with a powerless clawing. "I have no wish to weaken my father. I merely gave you the truth."

His gaze was filled with a bitterness that cut through her. "Your 'truth' is only useful to me if I can quote it to your father's face. Our fates are sealed no matter what you or I wish, no matter what skeletons we have in our closets."

Zohra's palms turned clammy. He was not backing out. Marrying a stranger, being locked forever into the cage of duty and obligation—the same duty that had ripped her family apart? She would take an uncertain future over that.

She sought and discarded one idea after the other, panic gripping her tight.

"Fine," she said, her mind already jumping ahead. It had been a waste of time to come here. "I have only one choice left then."

She turned around, determined to act before the night was up. She couldn't stay in the palace, in Siyaad for another minute.

She was about to step over the threshold when a hand on her arm pulled her back. A soft gasp escaped her mouth as she was pushed against the wall with sure movements. The muscles in her arms trembled, her senses becoming hyperaware of every little detail about him.

Like the strong column of his throat as his chest fell and rose. Like the tingle in her skin where his fingers touched her.

"I suddenly have great sympathy for your father, Princess. My sister Amira is just as headstrong as you seem to be, but at least, she listens when Azeez or I…"

A dark shadow fell over his face. He had spoken of his sister as though she was still alive. She shouldn't care about his pain, but it pierced through her anyway.

"Your sister? The one who died five years ago?"

He met her gaze. The pain in it flayed her open. "Yes."

His hands landed on either side of her face. He bent until she could see the light scar over his left eyebrow. Any grief she had seen a moment ago was gone. "Now, tell me what the only choice you have left is."

She pushed at him, but he didn't relent. "I've not given you the liberty to touch me, Prince Ayaan, neither to haul me around."

"You should have thought about that before you barged into my room, Princess." Mockery gave his mouth a cruel slant. "Whatever you do now, I will hold myself responsible for it."

"You wouldn't have even laid eyes on me until the wedding if I hadn't forced my way in here. No one is responsible for my actions or my life but me."

"I became responsible for you the minute I said yes to this alliance. And I won't let you cause any more problems for your father."

"This…" she couldn't speak for the outrage sputtering through her "…this kind of archaic behavior is what I'm talking about. Your claim just proves how right I am in wanting to get out of this marriage, out of Siyaad."

"So you're going to run away in the middle of the night and expose your father to a scandal?"

"I owe my father nothing. *Nothing.* And I'm not running away, I'm going to exercise my right as an adult and leave. Neither my father nor you can force me into a marriage that I don't want, nor can you stop me from leaving."

He took his hands away from her. Not trusting his actions even for a second, Zohra straightened from the wall. Her knees shook beneath her.

"Fine, leave," he said, displeasure burning in his gaze. "But you leave your father no choice either except to announce my betrothal to your sister. I understand she will be eighteen in a year."

Bile crawled up Zohra's throat and pooled in her mouth. How dare he? "*Sixteen and a half.* My sister is sixteen and a half."

Only silence met her outburst.

She covered the gap between them, fury eating away at reason. She pushed at him, powerless anger churning in her gut. Saira would never go against their father. She had been born and raised in Siyaad, exposed to nothing but the incessant chatter about duty and obligation despite Zohra's presence.

"You cannot do that. She…I won't let my father or you…"

She fisted her hands and let out the cry sawing at her throat.

There was nothing she could do to stop her father from promising Saira in her place. And he would, without blinking. Zohra knew firsthand the lengths to which her father could go for Siyaad.

Her chest felt as if there was a steel band around it, the shackles of duty and obligation sinking their claws into her.

"Saira is innocent, a teenager who still believes in love and happily ever after."

"And you?"

"They do exist. Just not in this world, in your world. And I will do anything before I let Saira's happiness be sacrificed in the name of duty."

"So you're not completely selfish then." He moved closer. "What is this world that I belong to, Princess, to which you don't?"

"It's filled with duty, obligations, sacrifice…what else? If Saira marries you, you will shatter her illusions, bring her nothing but unhappiness. You would marry a mere girl in the name of duty?"

Disgust radiated from him. "The very thought of betrothal

to a sixteen-year-old makes my skin crawl. But Siyaad needs this public alliance. Your father's heart attacks in the last six months, your brother's minor status, the latest skirmish at the border? It has made Siyaad weak. This wedding means that the world knows that Dahaar stands by Siyaad. It's the best chance your father, your people, have of retaining their identity. If something should happen to your father, your brother will have our protection.

"Knowing all this, you refuse this alliance? You risk your country's future, your brother's future by acting so recklessly?"

Zohra crumpled against the wall, the fight leaving her. She owed nothing to her father, nor to Siyaad. But Saira and Wasim…if not for them, she would have been so alone all these years. A stranger among her father's people at thirteen—shattered by her mother's death and the devastating truth that her father was not only alive, but that he was the sovereign of Siyaad and had a wife and six-year-old son and daughter.

If not for her brother and sister, she would have had nothing but misery. "I had no idea this would benefit Wasim."

"Why am I not surprised?"

His derision felt like a stinging slap. But this was all her fault.

She had always made it her mission to learn as little as possible about the politics in Siyaad, she had rebuffed her father's attempts to educate her, to make her active in the country's politics. If she hadn't sunk her head in the sand like an ostrich, she would have been better equipped to deal with this situation.

She ran a trembling hand over her forehead, shaking from head to toe. She was well and truly caught, all her hopes for a future separate from duty and obligation crumbling right before her eyes.

"If this is all for Siyaad's benefit, why are you agreeing to this? You can snap your fingers and find a woman who will be your silent shadow. You clearly already dislike me. You can still refuse this, you can help Siyaad without—"

"Enough!" Bitterness rose up inside Ayaan, burning in his blood like a fire unchecked. He reveled in the anger, in the way it burned away the crippling fear that was always lurking beneath the surface eating away the weight of what his lucidity meant to him. "You think you are anything like the woman I would want to marry if it wasn't for duty, if it wasn't to repay the debt my father owes yours?" he said, filling his every word with the clawing anger he felt.

Every inch of color fled from her face and she looked as if he had struck her. And Ayaan crushed the little flare of remorse he felt.

It would have been better if his unwanted wife had been a woman who would scurry at the thought of being in the same room with the Mad Prince. But this defiant woman was what fate had brought him.

There was no point in railing against it. "There is very little that matters left to me, Princess. Except my word. And I would rather be dead than lose that, too."

"Then, send me back when Wasim turns eighteen, when he doesn't need your protection anymore, however long that might take. The world will still know that Siyaad has your support. You can claim that I was an unsuitable wife and I will not contest you. You can sever all connections with me and no one will point a finger."

He shook his head, surprised at the depth of her anger toward their way of life.

To be rid of her when there was no need anymore was an infinitely tempting offer. But there would be no honor in it. "If I send you back, you will become the object of speculation and ridicule. That is a very high price for your freedom, Princess. It will always be tainted in Siyaad."

He saw the tremor that went through her, the fear that surfaced in her gaze. But of course, she didn't heed it. He already knew that much about this woman. "Anything is better than being locked in a marriage whose very fabric is dictated by duty and nothing else."

"Marriage to me doesn't have to be the nightmare you are expecting."

"What do you mean?"

"I have very little expectations of my wife. She will live in Dahaar. She will do her duty in state functions by my side. She will be kind and thoughtful to my parents.

"I will not love her nor will I expect her to love me. I don't even want to see her except in public. This marriage is purely for the benefit of my parents. And I don't care what you do with your time as long as you don't bring shame upon Dahaar. Our lives can be as separate as you or I want."

She frowned, her gaze studying him intently. "What about an heir? Isn't that part of the agenda that's passed down to you? Produce as many offspring, male preferably, as soon as possible?"

"How old are you, Princess?"

"Twenty-four."

"I thought I was too bitter for my age. I have no intention of fathering a son or daughter, Princess, not with you or anyone else, not until…" *Not ever if he didn't find control over his own mind.* "How about we revisit the invigorating subject of procreation in say…two years from now?"

She swallowed, drawing his gaze to the delicate line of her throat. "How do I know you won't change your mind… about everything?"

"I have enough nightmares without the added ones of forcing myself on an unwilling woman. Believe me, the last thing I want is to sleep with you."

Her gaze sparked with defiance. "If I'm to be stuck in a marriage that will save my sister and benefit my brother, then I might as well be in one with a man who's just as indifferent to it as I am."

Ayaan frowned, something else cutting through the pulse of attraction swirling around them. Not only had she elicited a reaction he had thought his body incapable of, but she had annoyed, perplexed and downright aggravated him to the extent that she had so easily banished the backlash from his nightmare, the chills he would have been fighting for the rest of the night.

That she was able to do that when nothing else had worked in the past few months rendered him speechless, tempted him to keep her there, even if it was only to...

Shaking his head, he caught himself. Whatever relief she brought him would only be temporary. "If you have had enough of an adventure, I will walk you back, Princess."

The smile slipped from her mouth, her gaze lingering on him, assessing, studying. She tucked her hands around her waist, loosened them and hugged herself again. Her indecision crystal clear in her eyes, Ayaan waited, willing her to let it go, willing her to walk away without another word.

Her gaze slipped to the bed and back to him, a caress and a question in it. Every muscle in him tightened with a hot fury. "Will you be okay for the rest of the—"

Forcing his fury into action, Ayaan tugged her forward. "Remember, Princess. You will be my wife only in front of the world. In private, you and I are nothing more than strangers. So stay out of things that don't concern you and I will do the same."

CHAPTER THREE

THE WEEK LEADING up to the wedding was the most torturous week that Zohra could remember, even though the wedding day dawned bright and sunny.

Prince Ayaan had left the next morning while Zohra and her family had traveled to Dahaara the day after that, renewed vigor seeping into her father who had been ill for the past month.

It was as though she could hear the ticking of the clock down to an unshakeable chain binding her to everything she hated.

With each passing moment, her confidence in her betrothed's words faltered, the midnight hour she had spent talking to him becoming fantastic and unreal in her head. Especially as Queen Fatima, Ayaan's mother, spent every waking hour regaling Zohra about Ayaan's childhood.

The contrast between the charming, loving boy his mother mentioned and the dark stranger she spoke to in the middle of the night was enough to cast doubt over everything.

Would he not expect anything from her? What kind of a man didn't even want to lay eyes on his wife?

She tugged the gold-and-silver bangles on to her wrists as the celebrations around the city blared loudly on the huge plasma-screen TV in her suite. The capital city of

Dahaara had been decorated lavishly, very much a bride itself, albeit a much happier one, ready for a celebration unlike Zohra had ever seen or heard of.

The gold-and-red-hued flag of Dahaar with the sword insignia flew on every street, from every shop. A holiday had been declared so that the people of Dahaar could enjoy the wedding. Gifts had been flowing in from every corner of the nation—breathtakingly exquisite silk fabrics, handmade jewelry boxes, sweets that she hadn't heard of before—each and every gift painstakingly overflowing with Dahaar's love of its prince.

The telecast of the celebrations, the crowds on the roads, the laughter on the faces of adults and children alike revealed how much this wedding mattered to Dahaar. The whole world was celebrating. Except the two people who were irrevocably being bound by it.

"Zo, look now. There he goes," Saira exclaimed, looking beautiful in a sheer silk beige dress that sparkled in the sunlight every time she moved. Zohra couldn't help but smile at the innocence in her half sister's voice. "Wow, Zo. I didn't realize he was so…handsome."

Unable to resist, Zohra turned and there he was.

Displayed in all his glory on the monstrous screen. The cameras zoomed in on him, and Zohra's breath halted in her throat.

Handsome was too tame a word for the man she was about to marry.

The motorcade transporting him and his parents weaved through the main street with ropes and security teams holding off the public.

Shouts and applause waved out of the speakers. It was almost palpable, the din of the crowd, the joy in their smiling faces. King Malik sat with Queen Fatima by his side, Prince Ayaan opposite them, resplendent in a dark navy military uniform that hugged his lean body, the very epitome of a powerful prince.

She could no more stem her curiosity about him than she could stop staring at him on the screen. Zohra shivered despite the sun-drenched room. He looked every inch a man who was used to having his every bidding done before it was given voice. Until she saw the detachment in his gaze.

Even through the screen, she could see the tension in his shoulders, in the tight set of his mouth, in the smile that curved his mouth but never reached his eyes.

He was standing in a crowd of people that loved him, next to parents who adored him, seemingly a man who had the world at his feet. And yet she could sense his isolation as clearly as if he were standing alone in a desert.

The joy around him, the celebrations, the crowds—nothing touched him. It was as though there was an invisible fortress around him that no one could pierce.

Did no one else but her see his isolation, the absolute lack of *anything* in that gaze? Would she have seen it if she hadn't seen him incoherent, and writhing in pain?

She swallowed and turned away from the screen. There it was—all the proof she had needed so desperately.

The truth of what he had said to her—that this wedding was solely for the benefit of his people, for his parents, was all laid out on the screen to see. Nothing but his sense of duty was forcing him to stand there, as it was forcing him to marry her.

The realization, instead of appeasing her, gave way to a strange heaviness that pervaded through her limbs.

She turned around, just as her father stepped into the room, dressed in the dark green military uniform of Siyaad.

She had done everything she could to avoid him once they had left for Dahaara. Busy as he had been in negotiations with King Malik and Prince Ayaan, it had been easy enough.

But, suddenly facing him in her bridal attire, the knot of anger she kept a tight hold on threatened to unravel. "Have you come to make sure I have not run away?"

Saira's gasp next to her checked the flow of bitterness that pounded through her veins. Passing a worried look between them, Saira excused herself, having never understood Zohra's antipathy toward their father.

"I know you're not happy with this alliance, Zohra. But I never doubted that you would do your duty."

There it was, that word again. It had broken her family apart, it had thrust her into an unknown world, and it had taken the life of her mother, who had done nothing but pine after the man she had loved.

She stood up from the divan and met his gaze. "I'm doing this for Saira and Wasim. I don't want Saira to be sacrificed in the name of duty, too."

He ventured into the room, and she braced herself for the impact of his presence. In the eleven years that she had lived in Siyaad, she had always stayed out of his way, made sure she spent the least amount of time with him.

"Is that what this marriage is to you? Can you not view it as anything else but sacrifice?"

"What else could it be? You didn't ask me if I wanted this. That man," she said, pointing her finger toward the screen, "didn't ask me if I wanted to be his wife. You have reduced my life to an addendum clause on a treaty."

His jaw tightened. "You will be the future queen of Dahaar, a woman who can have just as much power as she wants in the tri-nation region. Your education, your intelligence, they can be used to do good in Dahaar, Zuran and Siyaad, to pave way for new things, to change old ways, ways you have always called archaic. No one will ever dare question your right to rule along with Prince Ayaan. You will live the rest of your life with the utmost—"

"This alliance is nothing but a way to secure Siyaad's future."

He nodded, sudden exhaustion seeping into his face. "I am glad that Saira and Wasim mean something to you." *Unlike me*, the words hovered in the air between them. "That means you will at least keep an eye on them."

Zohra refused to feel guilty, refused to let him put her in the wrong when he had made an irrevocable decision all those years ago, when he continued to show again and again that Siyaad would always come first with him. "They are my family. I will do anything for them," she said, forcing herself to speak the words. "They are the only reason I've stayed—"

"In Siyaad all these years, I know."

The knot in her throat cut off her breath. She held herself absolutely still as he neared her, her gut twisting on itself. The sandalwood scent of him knocked her sideways, unlocking memories she had forcibly buried. Maybe if he had always been an absentee father, maybe if she didn't remember her mother's desolation, her own aching grief when she had been told one fine morning that her father was dead...

Only to learn after her mother had died that he had just walked away from them to take up the crown of Siyaad, that he had already had a wife.

His whole life with her mother and her had been a lie.

He pressed a kiss to her forehead, and the longing she fought broke free. But she couldn't let it out. If she did, it would hurt her like nothing else could. So she turned the emotion engulfing her into a bitterness that had already festered for so long.

"I always wondered why you took custody of me when

mom died instead of sending me to her brother. Living in Siyaad all these years, being a daughter, a bastard at that, I realized I have no consequence for you, no importance in your life. But now... Is this why? You knew I would come in handy for one of your many obligations toward your country?"

His mouth compressed into a tight line, a flash of anger in his gaze now. "When will you realize that Siyaad is just as much a part of you as it is of me?"

"Not in this lifetime."

Resignation settled over his features. And suddenly, he was the man who had had two heart attacks in the space of six months. "Whatever I say is immaterial because you've already decided the answer."

He clasped her cheek with his palm, his gaze drinking in every feature, every nuance in her expression. *He is remembering my mom.* Zohra knew that as clearly as if he had said her name out loud. Ever since he had suddenly reappeared in her life when she had been thirteen and dragged her to Siyaad, she had always understood one thing.

He had loved her mother just as much as her mother had loved him. And yet, he had walked out of their lives and put duty first.

"Ever since you were a little girl, you've always been stubborn. Incredibly strong but also stubborn.

"You've always decided your own fate, Zohra. You decided why I had left without ever asking me. You decided to hate your stepmother when you came to live in Siyaad, even though she had been nothing but kind to you. You decided you would have nothing to do with Siyaad or your heritage.

"*You* decided to love your half brother and half sister, *you* decided to stay in Siyaad for them when you turned eighteen. No one has or will ever tell you how to live your life.

"What you make of this marriage, whether you view it as a cage or your freedom is, as always, up to you."

Saira came bursting into the room, pink high in her cheeks. "He's arrived in the Throne Hall."

Zohra didn't need to be told again who it was that was waiting for her.

Her gaze anxiously shifting between Zohra and their father, Saira handed Zohra the bouquet of white lilies. Her palms were clammy as though she were walking to her execution rather than her wedding.

As the sweet scent of the flowers tickled her nose, Zohra took her father's offered hand. For a moment, she couldn't get her legs to move, couldn't shake off the sudden fear that descended over her.

In the next, she was standing at the entrance to the Throne Hall, a vast chamber with a high, circular dome ceiling. The moment Zohra and her father crossed the threshold, traditional Dahaaran music blared to life from their left and right. The festive sounds set her heart thumping in tune.

A gasp fell from her lips. The whole setting could have been torn out of her worn-out copy of *One Thousand and One Arabian Nights*. Back when she had still been enchanted enough to believe the magical stories spun by her father, before the reality of duty and obligation had shattered her world, before the truth of a princess's life had forced her to grow up too fast.

The hall was huge with at least a thousand gold-edged chairs on either side, leaving a carpeted path between for her to walk. The floor was cream-colored marble with inlaid jewels.

The carpeted path was strewn with red rose petals.

Zohra followed the path with her eyes to the other end of the hall, where there was a wide dais. Sheer gold-and-beige-colored fabrics draped across the dais which was built of steps leading to a gold-edged throne, wide enough for two. Thousands of cream-colored roses, with bloodred roses here and there, adorned every step and surface of the dais.

And standing next to the throne, his navy uniform contrastingly starkly against the richly romantic background, a blur to her panic-stricken gaze, was her bridegroom.

Never for a moment had she imagined such a lavish wedding, or such a forbidding-looking man waiting for her at the end of it. She had imagined the same day with Faisal so many times. A simple wedding free of obligations and duty with the man she loved, both of them able to live the life they had wanted.

How had such a simple dream turned into dust?

Her heart thudded hard against her rib cage, her chest incredibly tight.

Across the vast hall, her gaze met Prince Ayaan's. And held.

She had expected him to be just as isolated from her as he had been through the parade. And yet, she could swear he was tuned to her every step, every breath, as if they were the only two people in the huge hall.

Her nerves stretched tight at the intensity of that gaze. It burned hot, alive, intense and she realized she was the cause of it. That awareness between them, it had a life of its own across the vast hall.

Was he anchoring her or was she anchoring him onto a path neither wanted to go on?

Sucking in a breath, she severed the connection, and focused on something beyond his shoulder. An uncontrollable shaking took root in her.

She did not need his strength, imagined or real, nor did he need hers.

The setting of the wedding, the festivities and joy around her, it was all getting to her.

This marriage will be whatever you make of it.

For once, Zohra agreed with her father's practical advice and she intended to set the tone for it from the beginning. And that meant remembering the prince and she were nothing but strangers brought together by duty.

Ayaan heard Zohra's answer to the imam's question, her voice crystal clear with no hesitation in it. The second time and then the third time, she gave her consent to the wedding.

Whatever doubts she'd had, no one would detect even a hint of it in her voice right then.

Or that she was, in any way, not fit to be the future queen of Dahaar. After she had left that night, he had wondered not only at his father's decision to choose a woman with tainted birth—even if it wasn't her fault—but even more, someone as impulsive and hotheaded as her.

But had his father seen the strength and poise she radiated with her very presence as she did now? Had he seen the assertiveness, the intelligence that shone from her gaze? Had he thought Ayaan needed an educated, even an unconventional wife to compensate for...

Suddenly it was his turn to give consent and the imam's words washed over him.

He gave his consent, his promise to cherish, protect and love Zohra Katherine Naasar for the rest of his life, the words sticking in his throat.

Protecting her—that was the only promise he could keep and to do that, he needed to keep his wife as far from the reaches of his darkness as possible. He slipped an emerald ring, seated among tiny diamonds, onto her finger. And extended his own hand for her to do the same.

Her fingers trembled when they touched his, her movements betraying the anxiety she hid so well.

From everything he had learned about her, his bride belonged in a category of her own. And despite every warning aimed toward himself, he couldn't tamp down his curiosity about her. Especially as, for the first time in eight months, he could remember every sensation, every scent— every minute of his encounter with her in exquisite detail.

His days, especially hours spent in someone else's company, were usually a blur to him. Yesterday's groom's ceremony that his mother had observed with happiness glittering in her every movement was already a vague memory.

He'd had only silence to offer when his mother had told him how happy she was that he had accepted this alliance. For every hundred words she said, he had only one.

This morning had been the first time he'd faced Dahaar's people since his return.

He had choked in the face of the joy, in the expectations of the people of Dahaar and the crushing weight of it. They cheered him on, they called him a survivor, a true hero when the truth was he was fighting every waking and sleeping moment to stop his reality from turning into a nightmare.

It was how he saw his life stretch in front of him. Isolated during the day and fighting his demons each night.

Until his bride had stood at the entrance to the hall.

He had sucked in a sharp breath, feeling as though a fog was falling away from his eyes. Suddenly, he had become aware of the reverent hush of the crowd as they watched her walk toward him, the festive strains of traditional music and the scent of the roses around the dais wafting up toward him.

Instead of the pristine white that tradition demanded, her dress was of the palest gold color with intricately heavy embroidery. It draped her torso in a severe cut, even the neckline revealing nothing but the palest hint of her skin. Thousands of tiny crystals stitched into the bodice twinkled every time she moved. It was cinched at her tiny waist and then showed off her long legs. Her hair was piled high and atop it sat a diamond tiara.

He had no doubt as to what statement she was making with that dress. Subtlety in any shape or form was apparently a strange concept to his bride.

His mouth curved, a lightness filling his chest.

The severity of the style did nothing but highlight the shape of her body—every curve and dip neatly delineated to satisfy his spiraling curiosity from that night.

Her skin glowed. She wasn't the most beautiful woman he had ever seen. Her features were too distinct and determined to play well with each other, but in that moment, there was no woman who would have suited better to be the future queen of Dahaar.

The longer he took in her beautiful face, the faster his heart beat.

His gut tightened in the most delicious way, a slow curl of heat unraveling in his muscles. He shuddered at the strangely dizzying sensation.

When the imam completed his prayer and she turned to look at Ayaan, the scent of her skin—rose attar and something else—teased his body into rising awareness.

She was his wife, his woman.

In name only, but in that moment, the primitive claim washed away everything else.

The music climbed a crescendo and the imam pronounced them man and wife.

She was now Princess Zohra Katherine Naasar Al-Sharif, the future queen of Dahaar.

Cheers and good wishes swept up through the hall. He let it all flow over him, fighting the inimitable weight of it, willing himself to focus on the happiness flowing around.

Hooking her hand through his, he led her down the steps of the dais and toward the area on the right to where the next ritual would take place. She had asked for the ceremonies to be completed the same day.

"What was the reason for this request?" he whispered at her ear, noticing her eyes light up as her brother Wasim hugged her. She said something to him and immediately the young prince of Siyaad cheered up.

It was the only time she fully smiled—when it was her half sister or half brother. For the rest of them, including her father, there was never a smile, at least not one that reached her eyes. Only a distance she clearly projected between her and the outside world.

Pity, because her smile held inexplicable warmth, almost a promise to chase away the shadows from the person she bestowed it on.

She stilled and turned toward him, her hand going to the sheer, gold-colored veil that fluttered from beneath the tiara. He leaned in and tugged it from where it had caught on the tiny crystal on her bodice. His fingers grazed the curve of her breast. She jerked back just as he did.

Her beautiful brown eyes flared. "I have no love for rituals that take three days. This way, my father can return to Siyaad tomorrow morning instead of waiting for another three days and spend energy he doesn't have on—"

"I thought you didn't care about your father."

"I don't. But it doesn't mean that I want him to suffer. That would just…"

"Finally break through your stubborn head and show you what an ungrateful daughter you are."

Zohra came to a sudden halt and stared at the man who was now her husband. They were surrounded from all sides by her father's family and his own. And yet the scorn that had rattled in his words was just as obvious in his gaze. "Have I done something to upset you, Prince Ayaan?"

"No, Princess," he said, lingering a second too long on the title. "Just telling the truth as I see it. It seems very few people dare to."

"And you do?"

"I have taken an oath just now that I would protect you. Even if it has to be from yourself."

"And of course, being a man, you have all the correct answers without knowing anything about my relationship with my father, right?"

One corner of his mouth turned up in mockery. "Have you noticed how every argument with you comes down to the fact that I am a man and you are not? One would think beneath all this contempt you show for duty and Siyaad, you're just annoyed that you are not allowed to rule."

His arrogance rendered her mute for a second. "I have never coveted the crown of Siyaad," she said, angry with herself for letting him rile her so easily. "All it entails is that you endlessly sacrifice either your or your loved ones' happiness at its feet."

"As you are apparently unable or unwilling to see, I will spell it out for you, Princess. It seems your father has given you unfettered freedom while you didn't even blink at the idea of betraying his trust. A princess of Siyaad, spending her summers in the desert, falling in love, the very life you have led is a testament to it. You're standing here," he said, laying his arm so casually against her waist that for a moment she lost track of what he said, "for no other reason than because *you* think you're protecting your sister from a horrible fate."

Her father and now Prince Ayaan, had both said the same thing to her.

Did they not see that it was their devotion to duty that had left her with no choice?

After more than an hour of mingling with guests, either strangers or her father's family, who snubbed her or the courageous ones that veiled their insults cleverly, Zohra was to ready to escape when she found herself next to her new husband.

His nearness unsettled her, an extra layer of awareness sparking to life. Or maybe it was that he had a habit of saying things that burrowed under her skin.

A ten-layered white glazed cake that looked like a castle perched on the edge of a mountain was wheeled in front of them.

She laughed and turned toward him. "This has to be the best part of wedding a prince."

His gaze lingered over her mouth a fraction too long before he responded. "A lesser man would take offense at that, Princess."

His hand was callused and warm over hers as they cut the cake, his breath an unwanted caress against her skin. Maintaining her smile took more effort than it should have. "It's a good thing you're not a lesser man, or even the average. I didn't think it was possible for anyone to be so…"

The cheers around them should have fractured the intimacy of the moment. Instead, a web wove around them and neither could dispel it. His long fingers brought a piece of cake to her mouth, and Zohra's skin prickled. "So…?"

Swallowing the cake past a tight throat, Zohra mirrored his actions. His mouth, opening and closing over her fingers, sent a shiver up her spine. Shaking her head, she struggled to find her voice. "So unaffected, untouched by...everything around you. You seem to want nothing for yourself, you..."

"Who said I don't want anything?" he whispered.

His words washed over her like warm honey. Her gaze flitted to his lips as if drawn by a force she couldn't fight.

He really had the most sensuous mouth—full and lush, in perfect contrast to the sharp angles of the rest of his face. Longing, unbidden and powerful, reached and held tight inside her muscles.

With that awareness also came a gut-clenching realization. This man, despite all his promises of expecting nothing from her, was more dangerous to her than a traditional prince could have been. Because she didn't know what to predict from him. Like now.

Suddenly, a flicker of such unbearable pain filled his gaze and she lost track of her thoughts. He hadn't been fully smiling before—he never did—but at least there had been a gleam of indulgent humor in his expression. Now, his features were frozen into a cold mask.

A servant approached them with a long, rectangular silver tray in hand, the contents of it hidden under the Dahaaran flag.

Zohra could see the gleaming silver hilt of a sword encrusted with emeralds peeking from under the cloth.

"It is yours now, Ayaan," Queen Fatima said, her eyes filling up with tears.

Zohra turned toward him when no response came from Ayaan.

He looked at the sword as if it were something expressly

sent to torture him. There was a deathly pallor to his skin while his gaze remained glued to the tray.

Unease fluttering in her belly, Zohra looked to her new mother-in-law. For once, she was irritated at her own decision all these years to learn nothing of rituals and culture.

"Queen Fatima, what is the significance of this sword?"

"It was my brother's sword." The answer came from Ayaan, who was still staring at it. "The one he was honored with when he was announced the crown prince of Dahaar."

"I think Azeez," the queen began, "would have been happy to see you take it for yourself, Ayaan. And what better occasion—"

"What Azeez would have wanted was to be alive. As he deserves to be."

The words from Ayaan sounded like an anguished growl to Zohra. And she was sure she was the only one who had heard them.

In the next moment, Ayaan walked away without looking back, leaving a hall full of state dignitaries and distinguished guests staring after him with a mixture of curiosity and shock.

CHAPTER FOUR

AYAAN DRIED HIS hair roughly and threw the towel aside. He was bone-tired after his rigorous exercise regimen. It was the only way he knew of knocking himself out. Drown his body in so much physical strain that there was nothing for his mind to do but bathe him in sleep.

Sometimes it worked, sometimes he woke up screaming in the middle of the night.

At least he was in good shape. Khaleef, his bodyguard, a man he had known all his life, hadn't let Ayaan run to fat and utter worthlessness in five years. His mind might be out of his control, but Ayaan intended to retain every ounce of control over his body.

He came to a halt, facing the doors of his suite. He hadn't seen Zohra since he had stormed out of the Throne Hall.

He had been caught up in her beauty. But more than that, he hadn't been able to stop himself from pushing past her prickly armor and boundaries. The same boundaries that he had forbidden her to cross with him. And yet with her by his side, the joy of the festivities had made a mark even on him, reminded him of who he used to be five years ago.

And then he had seen his brother's sword. A stark reminder of why he was the one standing.

Several hours later now, the image of it refused to leave him alone. He pushed through the doors, came to the head of the bed and turned the light on. And stopped.

Wearing a gown made of the silkiest chiffon in the color of turquoise, Zohra lay sleeping against the pillows on his side. Instant heat swirled low in his gut. It was his wedding night, and his bride was sleeping in his bed. Even half the man that he was, he couldn't remain immune to the breathtaking beauty of the woman.

She slept on her back, her hands raised above her head. The swirls of henna across her skin were beautiful and his gaze swept over her body.

Her delicately arched feet were also decorated in the same deep red intricate design disappearing beneath the gown at her calves.

The dress swirled around her slender form and yet managed to drape silkily over every curve and dip. Over her legs and her thighs, over the indentation of her waist and finally over her breasts.

Hundreds of golden threads were worked around the neckline, the weight of which pulled the fabric down. Giving him a view of the upper curve of one breast. They were small and rounded and he couldn't move his gaze from the sight.

Desire ripped through him and even the simmering anger he felt at her presence couldn't wash it away. He moved closer without knowing it. She smelled divine, like roses and attar and a rich, erotic fusion of both with her own scent.

In eight months of lucidity, he had never once felt so alive, felt desire as sharp and focused as now. And he couldn't easily dismiss this sharp hunger at the sight of her, or view it with distaste.

Her long hair was fanned over his pillow, her mouth

pink. Long lashes lent her an air of vulnerable feminin-
ity that was missing when her eyes were open. Because
she was busy studying, assessing, challenging with that
intelligent gaze.

Suddenly, her gaze flew open. It stayed unfocused,
muddled with sleep. A slight flush lit her skin with a rosy
hue. Her gaze traveled over him lazily. Ayaan felt the force
of it down to his toes. For a second, all he could think of
was to climb into the bed.

Irritation flickered hot inside him. But he waited silently
for the heat of his desire to subside, even as he wondered
what had brought that smile to her lush mouth.

Shock flickering through her brown eyes, she shot up
and pushed her hair from her face. "Prince Ayaan, what
are you doing here?"

He raised a brow at her indignation. "That should be
my question. You're in my bed, in my suite, in my wing
again, Princess. If I were the jealous, possessive kind of
husband, I would take offense at how often you end up in
a man's bed."

Pulling herself up against the headboard, she looked
around, her gaze wide. It swept over his suite. Pink crept
upward from her neck. And the glare in her eyes went to
full-blown anger. She half slipped, half jumped from the
bed, her movements panic-stricken. "If you had been the
normal, entitled, king-of-everything-I-survey kind of man
like I had hoped, you would have rejected me and I would
be nowhere near this palace or you."

She turned around and started pulling the cushions and
pillows here and there. Bent over the bed like that, she gave
him a perfect view of the curve of her bottom draped by
nothing but the sheerest silk. The woman was capable of
pushing him over the last edge he was already standing on.

He grabbed his robe from the foot of the bed and threw it at her. "Cover yourself and get out of my chamber."

Zohra clutched the robe out of pure instinct while, she was sure, mortification turned her face bright red. "You think I want to be here, half-naked and incoherent, laid out like a feast for you?"

His silence in the face of her mounting fury chafed at her. She shrugged into the overlarge silk robe, the sleeves doubling over past her hands. "This is all because of your mother and her army of…"

The roaring blaze in Prince Ayaan's gaze, the concrete set of his jaw curbed her words. He took a menacing step toward her, his mouth flattened with fury. "Do you have no filter between your brain and your mouth, Princess?"

Mortification heated her skin like fire, but Zohra was damned if she left before she cleared his assumption that she wanted to be in his bedroom. "I have been awake since before dawn, going through a million rituals that mean nothing to me. I nearly fell asleep in that monstrous tub of perfumed oil before being led here," she said, meeting his gaze.

His hands folded at his chest, he stood there like a block of ice, unwavering, unfeeling. As though nothing mattered to him except his imposed isolation from everyone around him, as if his very survival was hinged on it. Frustration and curiosity turned Zohra inside out.

"I have no interest in how you arrived here, Princess. I do not want to see you in my quarters ever again. Is that understood?"

Zohra nodded, her own anger coming to her aid. It was what they had agreed upon for their marriage. But his cutting attitude, as if she polluted the very air around him by breathing it, reminded her of things she never wanted to remember. She lifted her chin, infused steel into her words. "I have no wish to remain here and bear the brunt of your uncivilized behavior. But I have no idea where I am supposed to go."

Her legs shook beneath her, a gaping void opening up in her gut. But she refused to let him see the nagging hurt his words evoked. He was not the cause of it, she knew that, but his words were a reminder of the most painful fact of her life. Since her mother had died, she had not belonged anywhere. Her life felt as if it was a repeat telecast of the worst moments; indifference and resentment. "Unless you want me to make a spectacle of myself and roam around the palace at this hour of the night in the inconsequential gown underneath this robe, I suggest you get off your high horse and find yourself a different bed for the night."

He reached her before she could blink, his hold on her wrist inflexible, leaving Zohra no choice but to follow. "As you might already be guessing with that smart head of yours," he said, his jaw so tight that she wondered that she could hear his words, "not only is the man you married uncivilized but he is also a coward who loathes sleeping anywhere but in his quarters."

Because of his nightmares?

Her chest tight, Zohra stared at his profile as he tugged her through the door. She swallowed the question, shrugging off the instant concern that stole over her.

She had no idea how far they had gone until they were standing in front of another set of doors. But by the thick silence around them, Zohra knew they were still in the same wing.

"This has to work for tonight."

With that curt statement, he turned and left, leaving Zohra speechless in his wake. Tucking her arms around her, she ventured into the huge room. Now that she was awake, the scent of attar and rose that clung to her skin cloyed through her, the sensitive rub of her thighs making her aware of her state of undress.

Using the velvet-covered footstool, she lugged herself onto the antique bed and lay down. She shivered, even though the room was comfortably warm. Silver threaded white cotton sheets rustled as she settled in, the silence creeping into her skin.

She stared up at the canopy of the bed, shameful tears pooling in her eyes.

Hadn't she lived through this same lonely moment too many times to be still weighed down by a stranger's indifference to her?

Zohra had known what she was taking on for Saira's sake and yet she couldn't shake the loneliness that twisted inside her, the crippling fear that she was bound to spend her entire life alone.

Stepping over the threshold of the State Hall, Zohra smiled for the first time in the week since the wedding. She was wearing an extremely comfortable and stylish pink pant-suit thanks to her personal stylist, and, for once, Zohra felt she could handle the day ahead.

It was the first official public event that Ayaan was attending since the wedding. Her gaze focused on Ayaan who, Zohra had noticed, rarely met his mother's eyes. Queen Fatima had walked them through every event that had been planned for the day. Even Zohra knew that it was a job for a political aide but she had a feeling the queen had taken it on so that she could spend some time with her son.

A small crowd had already gathered, including Ayaan's parents. Clad in a slate gray suit that hugged his wide shoulders, Ayaan stood at the opposite wall. His jaw clean-shaven, the unruly waves of his hair combed back, he looked every inch a commanding prince who had come back to Dahaar and its people against all odds.

He stood near his father and two other suit-clad men, but the way he stood, slanted away from the group, with a smile that curved his mouth but didn't touch his gaze, Zohra felt his isolation like a live thing, almost as if there were a fortress around him.

A hush fell around her as everyone noticed her entrance. Her skin prickled with awareness like a warning beacon just as those golden eyes landed on her. And she saw the infinitesimal tightening of his shoulders, the long indrawn breath, as if he were bracing himself.

Frowning, Zohra struggled with the overwhelming urge to turn tail and disappear. She already had a healthy amount of dislike for any state affairs, and Prince Ayaan's long-suffering attitude toward her presence on top of that grated at her.

She reached his side and the group widened to include her. Her nerves tightened at the press of Ayaan's hard muscle beside her and all she could hear was the amplified thud of her heart, the whistle of every hard-fought breath, as he introduced her.

Ayaan's palm lay against her lower back. She shivered, wondering if there was a brand on her skin in the shape of his palm. Zohra couldn't remember the names of the two men and their wives a second after they fell on her ears.

How could she react so strongly to his presence while he barely tolerated hers?

He turned her toward him slightly. "I hope you have recovered from the wedding, Princess."

A stinging response rose to her tongue. Pulling a deep breath in, she looked around and checked her impulse to shout at him in a very unprincesslike way. "You are actually deigning to speak to me?" she whispered.

He blinked at the animosity in her tone.

"Of course, state functions. That was in the rule book, wasn't it?" She was acting like a child, but she couldn't dismiss the image of Ayaan bracing himself to face her. Indifference and resentment had wounded her more than she had thought. And facing the same again...

"One of the times you will sigh deeply and suffer my company instead of banishing me from your presence."

His hands locked behind him, he studied her with an intense gaze as if he could drill into her head and read all her secrets and fears. His mouth flattened, his ire nothing but a spark in his golden brown gaze. "And here I was afraid that you were far too clever than I ever wanted my wife to be, Princess."

Rooted to the spot, Zohra stared at his back and spent the next two hours wondering what he meant. The informal social gathering complete, they were led through a narrow entrance, flanked by uniformed guards dressed in Dahaar's navy blue.

Surprised by the security measures, Zohra was about to ask Ayaan when huge, ancient doors opened in front of them.

It was a scene unlike Zohra had ever seen.

A roar went up instantly at the sight of Ayaan. They were in a marble-tiled hall, ten times bigger than the huge throne room with at least a thousand people standing upon the wide staircase on the other side and more falling into a single line behind security ropes around the perimeter of the hall.

With every cheer and greeting that came from the crowd, Zohra felt Ayaan freeze next to her, inch by painful inch as if someone was injecting ice into his very veins. She heard Queen Fatima whisper Ayaan's name, saw the king's concerned pat on his shoulder but Ayaan didn't budge.

He could have been the statue of a centuries-old warrior for all the life she felt in him.

Seconds merged and a tiny ripple of shock spread through the group around them. The cheers from the crowd began to pale into something else. Zohra stole a look at Ayaan and her breath hitched in her throat. His face looked as if someone had poured concrete over his features, his nostrils flaring as he fought to breathe.

Was this what he faced every time he walked in front of a crowd?

Her throat tight, Zohra reached for his hand. He didn't budge. She moved closer, clasped her fingers around his.

He turned and the distress in his gaze shook her insides. Shadows upon shadows flickered in the golden depths, mocking her petty insecurities and peevishness. She knew he wanted to leave, but she also knew he would castigate himself later.

Words came and fell away from her mouth, every one more trite than the previous. She couldn't even begin to imagine what he saw, or felt at that moment.

She shook her head with a tsk-tsk sound, strove to fill her words with a lightness that she was far from feeling. She tugged at his fingers, forcing him to focus on her touch, her words. "Is it because of my illegitimate birth or the fact that I lack a certain important organ that I have never been treated with half such enthusiasm in Siyaad?"

A lick of humor came alive in his gaze. "I would say a combination of both." The tight lines around his mouth relented. His gaze swept over her, wide, intense. "And more importantly, what they show you or not show you is only a reflection of your own interest in them, Princess."

Even with the black cloud of whatever it was that

haunted him, he didn't hold back his punches. She nodded, even though the truth stung. "Whereas you, they have known you your entire life."

He nodded. She heard him release his breath, felt him move closer to her until their sides grazed. "Except for the last few years."

"I thought turning back on something like this was nothing for a prince but it is not, is it?" she ventured.

She felt his gaze move over her, but stared straight ahead. Their fingers were still laced together, and yet there was no getting used to the feel of his rough fingers against hers. "No," he said after a long pause.

"What about this…bothers you, Prince Ayaan?"

He clamped his fingers tighter around hers. She must have made a sound because he instantly loosened his grip. "I'm not the man they think I am. I am not the man I thought I was long ago."

Zohra took in the eager anticipation on every face in the crowd. Standing so close to him, feeling the heat from his hard body, seeing him fight his fears with every inch of him, she had never been surer of a man's strength. "I have spent many moments in the past week accompanying you to various state functions that hold no meaning or significance for me, I have witnessed their celebration in your name. And I have come to understand one thing. They know exactly who you are, what it takes for you to be here and they accept you, Prince Ayaan. Even *I* know how rare that is."

It was only after the words had left her mouth that Zohra realized the very truth in them. Still, she braced herself for his mockery, expected him to laugh at her. Because, in reality, she was beginning to see how very little she knew about this life, and what it entailed.

He leaned down toward her, and she was enveloped by

the scent and heat of his skin. "You are a contradiction in yourself, Princess. I cannot quite decide whether the selfish, defiant version is the real you or this quiet, regal, perceptive one."

Shock robbing her senses, Zohra just stared at him. *Was she both or was she neither?*

She was still wondering the answer to that when Ayaan took a step forward and waved at the crowd. Their roaring response was earsplitting.

He turned around and looked at her. His gaze studied her as if solving a puzzle. And then instead of asking her, he tugged her forward until she had no choice but to walk by his side.

Be my wife at state functions.

It was one of the few things he had asked of her, and in this moment, Zohra couldn't shake off the feeling that it was her that Prince Ayaan saw and not a faceless, name-less woman he had married in the name of duty. And try as she did, the feeling wouldn't leave her alone.

They spent the entire day greeting Dahaarans who had traveled long distances to meet their prince and his new bride. And the hardest part was that all through the day, he kept touching her. He never completely relaxed but after the first hour, he became less tense.

Of course, Queen Fatima had warned her that there were eyes and ears watching their every move, hungrier than usual about the crown prince who was finally enter-ing the political arena of Dahaar and his first formal cer-emony with his new Siyaadi bride.

The little touches of his palm at her back, the brush of his hand against hers, were more for public display than anything else, but they affected her strongly nonetheless.

Her fingers tingled when he clasped them with his own, her heart thudded, every inch of her body thrummed as if they were alone instead of in a sea of people, as if he touched her because he craved it, because he needed to.

And despite her best efforts, Zohra kept forgetting that the man she had married sought nothing for himself. Not pleasure or power or fame.

The prince of Dahaar did everything he did in the name of duty.

CHAPTER FIVE

AYAAN ENTERED THE vast hall and took his seat opposite his mother while his father sat at the head of the centuries-old dinner table. And just as it did for the past few months, instantly his throat closed up, an unbearable stiffness setting into his shoulders.

The ancient, handcrafted table that probably weighed a ton, the colorful walls hanging with handmade Dahaaran rugs that showcased historical Al-Sharif events, the high circular ceilings... Every time he entered the hall, he felt as if he entered a tomb, as if he was being slowly but surely smothered by every inanimate object in the room.

Not to mention the fact he couldn't even look at his parents. Nodding at them, he settled into his chair. The weight of their attention was like a heavy chain on his shoulders.

Shying his gaze away from her, he answered his mother's inquiries about his day with single word answers, wondering why today felt even more painful than the past week.

The whole family together for dinner. Even before their family had been broken by tragedy, it had been a tradition his mother had enforced as much as possible. But never had it been such an exercise in pain as it had become since his return.

"Where is Princess Zohra?" his father asked, and Ayaan frowned.

Two weeks since their marriage, two weeks of countless political dinners and public appearances, and Zohra had somehow become the buffer between him and the outside world, even between him and his parents. Because whatever else his wife was, she was not a silent creature.

Listening to either her questions about the various ceremonies or her perceptive inquiries about state affairs and watching her struggle to curb her temper and her tongue—sometimes successfully, sometimes not—had become a daily ritual in itself. And looking at his father, Ayaan realized it was not just him that had become used to the princess's presence.

"Princess Zohra is completing the final wedding ritual and should be joining us any minute," his mother announced.

The uncomfortable silence descending again, Ayaan fidgeted in his seat, restless to leave. "Can we begin dinner?"

"No." An implacable answer from his mother which meant she was in full queen mode. It was a term his siblings and he had coined together.

His chest tightened at the recollection as Ayaan turned to the side and froze. One by one, the entire palace staff was entering the hall. The senior ones took their seats on low-slung divans along the perimeter of the wall while the rest of them stood in between. Almost a hundred of them and they were all dressed in their best, their pride and joy at being included shining in their gazes.

Another group of servants laid down numerous empty glass bowls with tiny spoons all over the huge table.

Straightening in his chair, Ayaan turned back to his mother. The restlessness in his limbs shifted, curiosity now rooting him to his seat. "What is the ritual, mother?"

"Every new Al-Sharif bride has to cook dessert for the family," his mother said, a hint of complaint in her tone. "Zohra somehow managed to postpone it until now."

Ayaan smiled. He could very well imagine Princess Zohra stomping with frustration somewhere. "But why is the entire palace staff here?"

His mother glanced in the direction of the entrance, the lines of her mouth tight. "They are all here to taste the dessert she cooks along with us, Prince Ayaan. It is a centuries-old tradition to give the staff a way to welcome the new bride, to give them a chance to feel that they are an integral part of the royal family."

Blinking, Ayaan leaned back against the chair. He had no idea if the Siyaadi princess could cook. For the first time in months, a strange anticipation filled him. But no matter what, he knew he was in for an interesting couple of hours.

Not just today, any time spent with his unconventional wife was always interesting. At the least.

He looked over to his right just as Zohra arrived at the entrance to the hall accompanied by fanfare and an army of excited servants.

Spying the anxiety in her gaze, the slight sheen of sweat on her forehead, Ayaan felt the most uncharacteristic surge of concern. From the corner of his eye, he could see Zohra approach the table with dragging footsteps that clearly said she wanted to be anywhere but here. In her hands was the centuries-old, gleaming silver bowl he remembered seeing long ago. Behind her, similar bowls were being carried by the kitchen staff and laid beside the low-slung divans where the palace staff were seated.

"Place the bowl on the table by Prince Ayaan's side, Princess Zohra." His mother's voice rang clearly in the deafening silence of a hundred and more curiously waiting gazes.

Her reluctance a tangible thing in the air around them, Zohra placed the bowl on the table next to Ayaan. A distinctive smell, sweet and...*burned*, wafted into the air around them.

His nostrils flaring, Ayaan glanced into the silver bowl. He gasped when he saw the contents, hearing the same sound fall from his mother's mouth and his father's cough. The dark brown, charred substance in the bowl looked like no dessert he knew.

His mouth twitched, and a sudden lightness filled his chest. Raising his head, he chanced a look at his mother. Her forehead tied into a frown, she was looking at the bowl with a shocked expression that had him clamping his mouth tight.

Whispers emerged from the staff around them, the more senior members even slanting a quick puzzled look at the bowl, but Ayaan couldn't help himself. Clearing his throat, which felt really hard, he looked up and met Zohra's gaze. "What is this, Princess?"

Her dark gaze fiery enough to burn him, she answered from tightly clamped lips, "*Halwa,* Prince Ayaan."

He didn't heed the warning in her voice. "You mean this is carrots and nuts?"

"Yes."

Fidgeting in his seat, he met his father's eyes at the head of table. Seeing the twinkle in his aged eyes, the tight set of his twitching mouth made Ayaan lose the tenuous hold on himself.

He laughed, the very act of it shaking his body from head to toe. And heard his father's peal of laughter alongside his own. His throat raw, Ayaan covered his face with his fingers but to no avail. His jaw and stomach hurt, but in the best way.

His body had no memory of what it felt like to laugh. Every face around them, including his mother's, watched him and the princess alternately, torn between the desire to laugh and bone-deep propriety.

Every time he looked at his father, it started again. He had no idea how long they laughed, but soon, he had tears in his eyes. "This is…" he choked, "*Ya Allah*, exactly like…"

His lean frame shaking with laughter, his father nodded, his mouth curled into a wide smile. "When Amira made—"

"When Amira made *Awwameh* on her twenty-first birthday," his mother finished, tears in her own eyes. Swallowing at the sight, Ayaan nodded, glad that her eyes were full of remembered laughter rather than the familiar shadows of grief.

"She hated every moment of it, too," his father said, looking at Zohra with a fond smile. "And Azeez and Ayaan teased her mercilessly for months."

A smile still curving his mouth, Ayaan met Zohra's gaze.

"Queen Fatima," Zohra's crystal clear tones rang through their laughter, laden with the promise of retribution, "who did you say tastes the new bride's dessert first?"

His laughter cut short, Ayaan shook his head and met his mother's gaze. "No."

Her mouth was still compressed but a spark of something wicked lit up his mother's gaze. "The husband, Princess Zohra," she said, studying him with an intensity that twisted his gut.

Zohra reached for a silver spoon, and scooped up a little of the charred *halwa* with it. "Traditions, of course, have to be followed. Do they not, King Malik?" she said, throwing the challenge at his father across the table.

Chuckles and approvals rang around the huge room, followed by his father's comment, "Of course, Princess Zohra," laden with laughter.

Knowing that he was well and truly caught, Ayaan looked up at Zohra. And opened his mouth when she brought the spoon to his mouth, victory dancing in her beautiful gaze.

When was the last time the palace walls had heard laughter like that? The last time his mother had smiled even if it had been buried under affected displeasure? The last time they had remembered the past with a smile?

With his chest feeling amazingly light, Ayaan reached Zohra's suite. The scent of scorched carrots and burned pistachios lingered in the air, bringing a smile to his mouth. He closed the huge doors behind him, suddenly craving the very privacy he usually avoided with her.

Leaning against the closed doors, he lost himself to the sheer pleasure of watching her. Cinched tight at her rib cage with a jeweled belt, the copper-sulfate-colored silk caftan she wore billowed from her tiny waist, highlighting the long line of her legs. The puckered sleeves showed off slender arms, the intricately designed diamond bracelets on her wrists twinkling in the light thrown by the lamps around the room.

She turned around, her hennaed hands tugging at the pearls threaded into her hair. The silky material cupped her breasts like a lover's hands, her stark sensuality robbing his breath.

Feeling like a teenager getting his first sight of a beautiful woman, he pushed away from the door.

He would ensure she was all right—a small courtesy

after the past two weeks—summon a maid, and leave. "Do you require help?"

She threw a quick look at the closed doors behind him and the slender line of her shoulders tensed up. "Have you not had enough fun at my expense, Prince Ayaan?"

He crossed the room and took her hands in his as she went to pull another pearl from her hair. Sensation skittered up his fingers, like a spark of fire. She wrenched them back right as he dropped them. "You do that a lot," he said, before he could think better of it.

"What?"

"Take your temper out on your beautiful hair."

It was a personal comment that shocked them both, instantly filling the air around them with tension. He had not intended to touch her, either.

"Why are you here?"

She had every right to question him and yet he couldn't turn around and leave. "I wanted to make sure you were all right."

"I am fine." Struggling with the clasp of the necklace at her nape, she glared at him. "Except for the small fact that I am now the laughingstock of the Dahaaran palace."

"I will pass a law that enforces the strictest punishment on anyone who dares laughs at you," he said, surprising himself again.

"Will it apply to the king and the crown prince?" she challenged. "Because as much as I would like to forget that image, it was your father and you that were laughing." Her gaze stayed on him, surprise in it, as if she couldn't quite believe what she had seen. "That sound is still ringing in my ears."

She dropped onto a divan with her feet stretched in front of her. Scrunching her nose, she grabbed the sleeve of her caftan, sniffed it and made a face. Ayaan clamped his mouth shut and rocked on his heels. She looked up at him, her mouth turned down. "Oh please, go ahead and laugh. I know you are dying to."

Ayaan laughed, the sound barreling out of him again. "I wouldn't have believed it if I hadn't been sitting there. You should have seen my mother's face when you put that silver bowl on the dining table. Centuries old, studded with intricate handwork, encrusted with rare gems and inside…" He hummed a dramatic tune.

Hunched over with her head in her hands, she groaned. *"It was not that bad."*

He dropped down onto the divan, still smiling at the expression on his mother's face, the twitch of his father's mouth. Silence in the grand hall had never held that much repressed laughter. "It was black and it tasted like soot, Princess."

She swatted him, her lower lip caught between her teeth, her beautiful brown eyes glimmering with laughter. "Have you seen the size of that palatial kitchen? How can anyone be expected to cook dessert for a hundred people? Of all the things I thought would make me unsuitable to be your wife…" Her eyes glittered like precious stones. "I…I thought I would be reduced to ash by Queen Fatima's glare."

"Even she cracked a smile at the end," he said, and Zohra doubled over laughing.

"For thirteen years, the palace staff at Siyaad were shocked by what I did but I think the faces of the staff here today…this is what they are going to remember for the rest of my life, aren't they?"

"I think it will be recorded as one of the most significant events in the history of Al-Sharifs." He stretched his hands wide, announcing the title. *"Princess Zohra and the Tale of the Burned Halwa."*

"As if this was the first humiliating ritual I have been forced to endure." She slid lower on the couch. "Even the ritual where I have to spend a week with you in the desert is—"

Cold skittered down his spine and Ayaan looked away. He had lost everything in the desert the night they had been attacked. He couldn't bear to go there again, not even for his mother and one of her rituals. "We are not going."

Noticing the shadows that entered his gaze, Zohra wondered what it was that she had said. Standing up from the divan, she tugged the pearls again, cursing the elaborate hairstyle.

"Stop that," came Prince Ayaan's voice closer than she had expected.

"I need to—"

His hands were suddenly in her hair, and Zohra's breath caught. The companionship of their shared laughter left the air around them and was replaced by something else. Her scalp prickled as Ayaan's long fingers untangled her hair with sure movements. She held herself rigid, so rigid that her back ached. The heat of his body behind her became a beckoning caress.

Closing her eyes, she took a bracing breath. How was she going to spend the next few years with this man when his simplest touch provoked this kind of reaction in her?

She was about to move away when his hands landed on her shoulders and pressed her toward him. Her pulse drummed in her ears, her skin shivering with a new awareness. Zohra gasped and turned around. His touch had been there one minute and gone the next, the pressure infinitesimal. But in that second, she had felt the shudder that had passed through his lean, hard body, heard the long inhale of his breath, as if...

"Forgive me, Princess," he said stepping back,

color riding those sharp cheekbones. "I shouldn't have touched you."

She clutched her arms against her body, frowning. His beautiful eyes were darkened like she had never seen before, his jaw tight. "Why did you?" she blurted out.

"You have known a man's touch, understand a man's hunger. Do you not know what a temptation you present, especially to one who hasn't been near a woman in six years?"

He muttered the last part softly, almost to himself. Yet the words landed in Zohra's ears with the same force of an earthquake. He was attracted to her and she'd had no idea.

"Six years?" she said, still reeling at the impact of his words.

There was a banked fire in his gaze, but the heat of it was still enough to send a delicious, feverish tremble into every muscle in her body. No wonder she felt so drawn to him, no wonder the air charged the moment they laid eyes on each other. "I never had a chance to fully explore what life had to offer a prince seeing that I was captured just before my twenty-first birthday."

Fierce heat tightened her cheeks. "Does that mean you've never..."

He frowned. "I was twenty-one when I was captured, not sixteen. I was never the one that women flocked to, like Azeez had been, but I have vague memories. The first time, it was..."

She slapped her palm over his mouth, loath to hear all the details. Desire bloomed at the sensitive skin of her palm, spreading through her entire body. "I don't want to know," she whispered, past a dry throat.

He pulled her hand off his mouth. "I didn't realize what else my madness had robbed from me until you showed up, Princess." He slowly peeled his fingers off her skin.

And Zohra realized with a thudding heart how much he didn't want to, what it cost him to let go of her.

A shiver shook her from within. For the first time a tendril of fear uncurled itself. A fear of the tightly leashed desire in him, and worst of all, her own reaction to that all encompassing hunger.

Tugging her hand back, she stepped away from him. And his unblinking gaze took in everything.

He moved toward the door, coming to a stop and turned back. The right corner of his mouth tilted up into a lopsided smile that wound itself around her. "I recommend a bath to get rid of that burned smell, Princess. Probably a rose-scented one." He looked gorgeous, the ever-present shadows of pain and grief temporarily gone. The tension in the room broke even as her body still remembered the imprint of his fingers on her. "As for all the rituals you have to suffer through, I appreciate you humoring my mother. The last few months…have not been easy on her."

Zohra had to grip the bed behind her to steady her legs. "I must admit, it's worth smelling like burned carrots to see you smile, Prince Ayaan. I see why the queen mentions it so much."

"Does she?"

There was such naked hope, such a hunger for more, in his gaze that Zohra couldn't draw breath for a second. It was a glimpse into the boy he must have been, the one his mother couldn't stop talking about. "Why do you sound so surprised? You are all she talks about."

He gave a tight nod, and leaned against the closed door, the levity gone from his face.

Hundreds of questions pummeled through her head. "Did she not know you were alive?"

The look he shot her was scorching.

She pushed off the bed.

The quiet swirled and snarled around them. His jaw tightened; his hands turned into white-knuckled fists. The silence went on for so long that she wondered if he would answer. It felt as if she was standing on the shifting, sinking floor of a desert. The more she tried to hold herself at a distance, the more Prince Ayaan and Dahaar wove into the fabric of her very life.

"Only my old bodyguard, who found me, and my father knew that I was alive. Khaleef roamed the desert for months without giving up. Even after the rescue efforts had been called off. I think he wanted to find our bodies for my parents."

The image those words conjured twisted her gut. "Did he?"

"No, but he did find me." He met her gaze then and Zohra heard the thread of anger in his. "Is this just puerile curiosity, Princess, or is there a point to this conversation?"

Her breath hovered in her throat, an intense tightness in her chest. She could give the easy answer—lie and face his scorn at what he termed curiosity. But she couldn't be a coward while facing the truth of her own feelings or fear.

Maybe if she heard what had happened to him from his own mouth, if she knew what tormented him, she could stop speculating. Maybe she would fear him and this... rampant, unwise curiosity about him would die away. Still, it was the hardest truth she had ever given voice to. "I think, as your wife, irrespective of our...true relationship, I have a right to know what I'm dealing with," she replied, not holding her punches back. "That sounds like I'm hinting something like the rest of the world is, but I would rather know the truth."

A flash of something lit up his eyes. She released the breath she was holding. "Hint, Princess? I don't think you know the meaning of the word."

He smiled, a genuine curve of his mouth, a banked fire-work in his eyes. It cut grooves in his hollowed-out cheeks and sent a pang through her gut. "I—"

"It's the first sensible thing you have said since you stormed into my suite." He turned away from her. "Khaleef found me in the desert, a couple of months after the attack. According to him, I…" She saw him swallow with great effort. "I was incoherent and violent when he approached me. He didn't let me out of his sight until he could per-sonally alert my father. My father took one look at me and sent me off to a castle in the heart of the Alps, where I was conveniently and blissfully mad for five years."

His words were so matter-of-fact, even when they held so much pain, that Zohra couldn't even speak for a few minutes. "Mad?"

He stared at her, as if suddenly realizing that she was there. "Mentally ill, violent, incoherent."

"Do you…remember what happened after you were captured?"

This time, there was no hiding the pain even in his stark face. "Most of it has come back to me."

"In your nightmares?"

He nodded, a flash of surprise in his gaze.

"So your mother had no idea that you were alive all these years or what…you have been through?"

He shook his head.

What had happened to him in the desert? What horrors did his mind revisit in those terrible nightmares?

Zohra hugged the strange fear that gripped her gut. She didn't want to know, not because the truth of what had been done to him would scare her. Maybe it would, maybe it wouldn't. But she was terrified of her own reaction, of crossing over a threshold and stepping into a path from which there was no return. Instead, she asked him something that had been bothering her, something that needed to be said even if it meant incurring his wrath.

"You said you were doing this—" she moved her hands to encompass them "—for your parents. But what's the point if your behavior is hurting your mother?"

He looked genuinely shocked, his frown deepening. Pure anger flattened his mouth and he took a step toward her. "*You* are lecturing me about duty toward one's parents? You've got a nerve."

Zohra refused to back down, even though his words hit her hard. "I've spent the better part of two weeks humoring your mother, seeing everything she hides from you and your father. Do you know that she hasn't spoken to him since you....*returned*? She feels so…"

Every time she looked at Queen Fatima, at the repressed pain in her eyes, Zohra's own pain, her mother's desolation after her father had left, it all rose to the surface. Lies, even told with the best intentions, caused pain much more terrible than truth itself. "I have seen the tears she hides from you and your father."

His skin lost pallor as though she had delivered him a physical blow.

"And yet you...*avoid* her. You barely exchange two words with her. She is standing on the outside, looking at you, wondering what she has done that you won't even—"

"How can she think she has done anything wrong?"

"Then why won't you speak with her, why won't you even meet her gaze?"

"*Because I'm not my brother.*"

It was a low growl that made the hairs on her neck stand up. His lean frame trembled as though he struggled to contain his emotions within. "I can't bear to look at her because when she sees me, she's looking for Azeez. She's remembering him, searching for something of him in me."

Zohra swallowed at the anguish in his words. "She thought all three of you were dead. She made peace with it until…suddenly five years later, she's told you're alive and…"

"Half-mad and haunted?"

"Your father had no right to lie to her."

His gaze flashed at her daring. "My father was protecting her. For all intents and purposes, *I was dead.*"

"He lied because it would not serve Dahaar's interests. This is what I hate about this life…about…" She had to stop to breathe through the tightness in her chest, to swallow the rage sputtering through her. *This was not about her.* "Resenting her for remembering your brother only makes you human. It doesn't mean she—"

"You think I resent her for remembering her firstborn? My brother was the golden prince, the perfect heir. Passionate about Dahaar, smart, courageous, a man who was everything the future king needed to be.

"I'm not him. He should have been the one that survived. That's what my parents think when they see me, that's what the cabinet, the high council think when they see me."

It was what he thought, why he was so isolated from everything and everyone, Zohra realized, shaking. How could anyone live with so much self-loathing, with so much pain tied into their very existence?

"Who gets to decide who should survive—"

He clasped her cheek, his hand gentle in contrast to his face, a stony mask. "You think I should be grateful that I'm alive? A broken man, a coward afraid of the dark? If it had been Azeez who had survived, he wouldn't have lost his mind for five years and hid in some Swiss castle, leaving my father to deal with the catastrophe. He wouldn't have regained his lucidity only to be haunted by memories."

The bitterness in his words leeched every ounce of heat from the room. The hairs on her neck stood up, her gut gripped by the tight fist of pain.

His pain. She could feel it seep into her, enveloping her.

"My brother would have taken up the mantle of Dahaar instead of still hiding behind our father. He would have chosen a woman like you for his queen instead of being forced into it by duty." His gaze swept over her mouth with a hunger that shocked her. "He would have been man enough to make you his wife in every way instead of hiding under a sham.

"Do you understand why I can't bear to look at her, Princess, why I can't bear to be near you? Because I'm not fit to be a son, or a husband, much less a prince."

Pushing away from her, he left the suite, leaving the echoes of his anger and pain swirling around her.

With her knees buckling under the weight of his confession, Zohra slid to the seat behind her. He was like a tornado, and as much as she wished to stay out of his path, she had a feeling he would suck her into him.

His laughter and pain carved places inside her. The truth of his desire that she hadn't been able to see until now thrummed through her. How could she have when she had been mourning Faisal's loss, when she was nothing but a figurehead in Prince Ayaan's life?

She needed to escape from him, from everything he unraveled within her by his mere presence.

CHAPTER SIX

ZOHRA TOOK A sip of the sherbet and forced herself to savor the cool slide of the liquid.

It was hard with a dozen pairs of eyes trained on her from every corner of the vast hall, each speculating why she was attending the first gathering in Siyaad after her wedding alone. If it had been up to her, she would have canceled it. But of course, the traditional Al-Akhtum gathering was even more important this year as her family needed to meet the crown prince of Dahaar and understand that he was now an integral part of Siyaad's politics.

Only she had left Dahaara without waiting to know if Prince Ayaan could fit it into his busy schedule or not.

There was something about being near him, even for a limited time, that unsettled her. Something that had burrowed beneath her skin and refused to dislodge. And it wasn't just the explosive desire that he had let her see.

By sheer force of will, she forced a smile as another of her father's cousins took in her attire from top to toe and made his displeasure the known. Although she wore a designer pantsuit with a long-sleeved jacket that covered up every inch of skin, it was still not the traditional caftan that Siyaadi women wore.

She'd heard the whispers behind her father's back, seen the sneers beneath the smiles, felt their snubs for eleven years. But her wedding the future king of Dahaar and the absence of her father today meant the claws that were usually sheathed were now out.

She could just imagine the whispers if Ayaan let her go in a few years. Whether her father was alive or not, whether Wasim was crowned the prince or not, her life would not change.

Would she resent Wasim and Saira as the years went on because her love for them held her back? Shuttling between Siyaad and Dahaar, a daughter but not a true one, a wife but not a true one. Nothing in her life held any significance, not to her, not to anyone else.

She was so tired of having no one to laugh with, no one she could even call a friend, of living each day with no sense of purpose or hope for a fleck of future happiness.

The depth of her loneliness choked her.

Zohra stiffened as the son of her father's cousin, Karim, came to a stop beside her. He was the most vicious of them all, hungry for the power of the throne, unhappy that her father had formed an alliance with Dahaar.

He blocked her against the table and leaned in a little too close.

"My sympathies, Zohra." The false sympathy in Karim's words coupled with that ever-present seediness made the hairs on her neck stand to attention. She knew what he thought of her. Easy. Whether it was the accident of her birth or the fact that she didn't simper and bow like a traditional Siyaadi woman didn't matter.

"I knew this would happen," Karim said, standing scandalously close. "I warned Uncle Salim that no one could be expected to accept *you* as his wife, even the Mad Prince."

Her stomach churned just hearing Ayaan spoken of like that. "You're not fit to utter his name."

Shaking his head, he smiled. "Tell me, Zohra. Why

did he parcel you back to Siyaad after only three weeks
of marriage? Has he already figured out you are...*unfit*
to be even a madman's wife?" He made a tsk-tsk sound
that scraped her nerves. A deathly silence fell around her.
Could everyone hear the filthy words that fell from his
mouth? "Is this because he discovered you are the result
of your mother's affair with a married man or because he
has discovered your own...*adventures* into love?"

The not-so-veiled threat in his gaze curled into dread she
couldn't shake. That her past could sully Prince Ayaan's
family's name sent feral fear pulsing through her. Not when
he had been nothing but honorable toward her, offered her
nothing but respect. Ayaan had challenged her, pushed
her buttons, surprised her with his sense of humor, but
not once had he treated her with anything but honor. The
realization stupefied her even as Karim leaned in closer.

"All I ask is that we be mutually beneficial to each
other." Bile scratched her throat. "And remember, Zohra,
I am always here when you need comfort, comfort that the
Mad Prince should be—"

Long fingers that looked extremely familiar curled
around Karim's shoulder, cutting off his words. Zohra
turned so hard that she had to grab the table behind her
to keep her balance.

Ayaan stood next to her, cold fury stamped over his
features. He bent his head toward Karim, but his gaze
collided with her own, unasked questions in its golden
depths. "Stand within a mile radius of my wife again and
you will regret it. Deeply."

He hadn't spoken loudly yet his voice carried around
the room. The color fled from Karim's face, leaving pasty
whiteness beneath the dark skin. "Prince Ayaan, allow me
to welcome—"

"Run as fast as you can, Karim."

The older man cast one last look at her and left the hall. Prickly silence shrouded the hall. Zohra breathed hard, her gut twisting and untwisting.

When had she become everything she detested? A useless princess waiting for her prince to do the saving?

She had known there was a chance Ayaan would be here. But she had been so caught up in her own misery to answer Karim back.

And now she was beholden a little more to the man she wanted to maintain distance from.

Standing so close that she could smell the scent of his skin beneath his faint cologne, Ayaan clasped her wrist gently. Their gazes met and held, the ever-present currents of desire arching into life. She could see the puckered scar over his eyebrow, hear the slightly altered tempo of his breathing.

His gaze missed nothing, the banked need in it reaching out to her. "Are you okay, Princess?"

This isn't about you, Zohra reminded herself sternly. If she had learned one thing in three weeks of marriage, it was that Ayaan bin Riyaaz Al-Sharif would have come to any woman's aid in the same situation. Honor was in his blood.

"I am fine," she finally managed to mumble. "And please, will you stop calling me that?"

He bent closer to her, the whole room watching them with bated breath. His brows pulled together, his gaze held a question.

"If you are waiting for me to thank you for coming to my aid so heroically," she said jerkily, hating that the crushing loneliness she had felt mere minutes ago disappeared in his presence, "you will be waiting for a while."

Leaning against the table by her side, he folded his hands. "Would you like to leave?"

She blinked. He was smiling. It was a wacky, co-conspirators kind of smile that barely curved his mouth. And yet it was there. The beauty of it was enough to scramble her already frazzled wits. "I...You are here to bestow all these people with the gloriousness of your exalted presence." She looked around the hall. "Leaving now would hardly accomplish that goal."

He turned away from her and she took the chance to study him greedily.

He wore black jeans and a white, long-sleeved tunic with a Nehru collar, handspun with the utmost care by the craftswomen in a small village near Dahaara specifically for their prince. The sleeves were folded to just below his elbows, a gold-plated watch adorning his wrist.

The collar was open at the neck, giving her a view of a strip of golden bronze skin. Feeling a flush creep up her neck, she turned away.

He was the most casually dressed man in the hall and yet a thrumming energy vibrated around him. It was a cruel joke indeed that he didn't realize the sense of power he wielded with his very presence. And it had nothing to do with being a prince either. From all the stories she had heard from his mother, Zohra knew he had once been laid-back, the one who had made everyone laugh, the one who had been the palace staff's favorite.

But he was more than that boy had ever been. Whether it was the torture he had been through or the responsibilities that lay on his shoulders now, Prince Ayaan was a formidable force in his own right.

He extended his hand toward her, palm up, cutting through her thoughts. She stared at the long fingers that always felt sinfully abrasive against her skin. "Princess?"

She raised her head and his gaze drank her in hungrily, as though he had been just as starved for the sight of her as she had been of him. "What is the point of being the Mad Prince if you can't at least postpone meeting the people you dislike?"

She laughed. The exaggerated arrogance in his gaze, the to-hell-with-it attitude of his words, it was knee-buckling. This was how he must have been before he had been captured.

A cocky, fun-loving prince who had been loved by everyone.

He straightened, his gaze unmoving from her face. "Why didn't you shut his filthy mouth?"

What could she say? That being amid her father's family made her feel like a lost and heartbroken thirteen-year-old girl again? That they had a way of punching her in the gut with the saddest truth of her life?

She didn't belong anywhere.

"You're the daughter of a king, wife to a crown prince. And more than that, you are..." Her heart crawled into her throat as he raked his gaze over her, "...*you, Zohra.*"

You are...you, Zohra.

He hadn't mocked her or called her princess.

His words washed over years of hurt, warming the cold, hard pain that had become a part of her. Her heart swelled, even the shadow of Karim's words, the bitterness of being here couldn't dilute what Ayaan's simple words meant to her.

Blinking back tears, she placed her hand in his. Her steps faltered, the strong clasp of his fingers around hers felt incredibly good, in more than one way.

She held her head high. It was borrowed courage, she knew that. But in that moment, she took everything the man next to her lent her.

The aunts and uncles and cousins were people who were related to her by blood, who should have been a source of comfort to a grieving girl but saw nothing past the circumstances of her birth. She finally had a chance to turn her back on them.

The moment they entered the corridor, the walls lined with portraits of the esteemed ancestors of the Al-Akhtum family, he stopped her. "I want an answer to my question, which you very cleverly evaded."

She shrugged. "They have called me names for eleven years, much nastier than today. Nothing I say or do today is going to change that. My stepmother's family hates me because I represent the pain my father caused her. And now they think I have stolen Saira's chance to be the queen of Dahaar. To my father's family…I am nothing but a taint on their lineage, a taint he dared bring to Siyaad. My father is responsible for whatever I face today."

"Does he know how they speak to you?"

"What would he do even if he did? Go back in time and stop having an eight-year-long affair with my mother? Change his mind about walking out on her when it was time to be king? Change his mind about taking custody of his bastard?"

His fingers tightened over her arms. "Stop referring to yourself as that."

She felt a hot sting at the back of her eyes. She was not going to cry just because someone finally had a glimpse into what eleven years of her life had been. She didn't need his pity. It only weakened her. "Powerful as you are, you cannot change the truth."

"What about the threat that Karim made? This man you were involved with…do I need to find Faisal? Is he the kind to—"

Foreboding inched tight across her skin. "How do you know his name?"

"You are my wife. Knowing everything about you, especially—"

"Especially what?" she said, swallowing the distaste his words brought back.

His expression intractable, his aristocratic features reminiscent of centuries of powerful lineage, he was every inch the arrogant prince in that moment. "Especially anything that could come back and cast a bad light on you and Dahaar, I have to know about it. I have to be prepared."

The same past that she had shamelessly used to try and get out of this marriage to him now curdled in her stomach. "Are you regretting your decision to not listen to me when I warned you? Wondering if you should sever all ties with me and leave me here in Siyaad?"

"I made my vows. Nothing will make me turn my back on them."

His words cut through her sharper than if he had said he had regrets. "Of course, your blasted word. Nothing in the world is allowed to interfere with it. How much detail do you want? How I met Faisal? Why I fell for him? How many times he—"

He thrust his face closer, bracing his hands on the wall on either side of her. His breath fanned against her skin. "My lucidity is nothing but the barest veil over my madness as you very well know, Princess." His words were low, gravelly, and instead of scaring her, they incited the most dangerous tingle in her blood. "Do not provoke me. You don't want to see what an animal I can become." He pushed back from the wall, as though he found her nearness suddenly distasteful. "All I need to know is if he is a threat."

She laughed, bitterness tinged into the sound. "He is not. I'm not the woman he wanted me to be."

His frown deepened. "You're pining after a man who cared

about the circumstances of your birth? I'm disappointed in you, Princess."

She shook her head. It was tragic how she was surrounded by men with highest codes of honor and yet they inevitably hurt her. "He didn't. As luck would have it, Faisal was nothing if not full of honor. When he learned who I was, he thought I should be grateful that my father acknowledged me as his daughter. He thought I should become this paragon of virtue and spend the rest of my life proving to Siyaad and its people that I was worthy of being a princess.

"He thought I should embrace my duty. He wanted to live in Siyaad, wanted to earn a place by my father....the list was endless. When I suggested we leave Siyaad as he had been planning before he met me, he looked at me as though I had committed the greatest sin. He left without saying goodbye."

The corridor echoed with the bitterness in her words, the silence filling up with her anger.

"Then you're the one responsible, aren't you?" he said, a hard edge to his words. "Not your father, or anyone else. *You* ruined your happiness."

A dark fear inched its fingers around her heart. "All I wanted was to leave this place," she said, speaking past the thick lump in her throat. "I would have gone anywhere with him."

"Maybe he realized your hatred for this life was more than your love for him? That he was just the excuse you needed to finally leave?" Ayaan delivered the words with a quiet ruthlessness, leaving her with nothing to hide under.

"Why are you being deliberately cruel?" she said, tears coating her throat.

His mouth curved, a bitter mockery of a smile. "I am returning a favor. Truth. It is the only real thing between us, isn't it? You tell me the truth that everyone else around me is too scared to voice for fear of making me mad again, and I do the same.

"If you had truly loved him, Princess, would it have been such a hardship to live with him in Siyaad?"

She shook where she stood, everything inside her balling up into an unbearable knot in her stomach. Ayaan became a blurry form as he turned away.

She had been so angry with Faisal for not taking her away, so heartbroken that he would put her status in Siyaad, and all it entailed, before her.

I won't be the one who will steal you away from your fate, Zohra. Those had been Faisal's words.

She grabbed the wall behind her, knees shaking under her.

Can you not view it as anything but a sacrifice?

Her father's words pricked her. Was she, once again, clinging to her stubborn anger and letting life pass her by? Was she going to spend the rest of her life waiting for someone to save her, as Ayaan had done just now, instead of saving herself?

CHAPTER SEVEN

AYAAN LEANED AGAINST the hip-length wall on the roof terrace, letting the peace and quiet steal into him. But even with the rooftop lit up, the dark black of the night seeped into his blood, working its shadows on him. He hadn't seen Zohra after yesterday, not even at the dinner with her family just now.

He hadn't wanted to inquire after her in front of King Salim and upset his already frail health. But after seeing the pain she hid from her father, the utter loneliness he had spied in her gaze, he didn't want to leave for Dahaar without seeing her.

He should have kept quiet about the man she had loved. But he had told her the bitter truth. Because the alternative had been to let her believe that she hadn't been loved. And he just couldn't do that.

A wave of possessiveness, selfish and unyielding, hit him hard. Did she still love that man? Was she even now bemoaning his loss somewhere in the palace?

His unwilling wife had left an indelible mark on the palace in just a few days, and more importantly, on his life.

In such a short space of time, Zohra had seen the truth, while his mother and he had struggled, danced around the issue, caused each other immense pain because they had each thought they were doing the best for the other.

Ayaan had endured the torment of seeing his brother's things, the medals from his military service, his degrees, the sword he had been presented, he even lived in the wing that had been specifically designed for Azeez when he had been crowned.

Because he hadn't wanted to hurt his mother.

But he couldn't bear it anymore, not when being near them stifled the breath out of him. So he had finally told her last night.

Ayaan had stood stiffly at the entrance to the day lounge she used, like one of the old iron-armored soldiers that adorned the palace, unable to move, unable to look into her eyes, terrified that she would touch him or even worse embrace him.

She had come to stand by him, and stopped suddenly as though realizing what her nearness did to him. "I will arrange a different wing for Zohra and you, away from the old ones. I only…want you to be happy, Ayaan."

To which he had nodded, incapable of answering, and walked away without a backward glance. Even though, for once, he hadn't felt like a pale shadow of his brother, hadn't felt the ball of guilt around his neck.

There were still things unsaid between them; her grief and his isolation were indefensible walls. But in that moment for the first time in eight months, the tight band around his chest had eased a little.

And he owed it to Zohra.

Every time he saw her, a little bit of his hold on himself loosened, forever vanished in the face of his escalating need to touch her. The need to feel like he could connect with at least one person in the world, to feel like he wasn't one man standing in the midst of a desert, alone. It was a dangerously seductive need.

Which was why he was standing here, waiting for his errant wife instead of on his way back to Dahaar.

He looked up as she appeared on the other side of the roof. A long-sleeved white shirt hugged her upper body, tucked into cream-colored jodhpurs. The outline of her torso, the long line of her thighs made his mouth dry up.

There was a strain on her features which fractured the mask of strength she donned so easily. She had left for Siyaad without a word to him, exactly as they had agreed. But her sudden disappearance had rankled more than he liked.

She stayed there, her gaze widening gradually.

He looked around, noticing what she saw. The rooftop glittered with hundreds of tiny, artistic lanterns lighting up the vast expanse, throwing orange packets of light everywhere.

A small table stood at the center of it, a traditional one of low height. A myriad of desserts sat atop it on silver plates, a silver jug with intricate patterns next to it. Two divans with plump cushions were placed either side of the table.

It looked incredibly romantic. A setting he himself would have orchestrated in another life. And he hadn't noticed it until Zohra had joined him, as if she was the only one who could awaken things in him that were not for mere survival.

He reached her side and leaned against the wall, smiling at the stiff way she held herself.

Finally, she met his gaze, extreme wariness in hers. "What is all this?"

"I asked Saira to summon you here to meet me. And that we were not to be disturbed." He looked around himself. "Apparently, Saira has a very active imagination."

"And I have no idea how to wake her up to reality," she said, shaking her head.

"Is it so unbelievable that for Saira, this life, this reality might not be so bad, Princess? Amira's wedding had been arranged, too. And I know that she was extremely happy. If you love Saira, you have to accept her reality, too."

She nodded without argument, her expression thoughtful.

"How long are you staying in Siyaad?" He hadn't realized he even wanted to know until the words left his mouth.

She frowned. "I checked with your assistant *and* mine before I left. There were no state functions or ceremonies that needed my—"

He cut her short, irritated with himself. "It was a casual question."

"Oh." Her frown didn't ease. "I thought you were flying back to Dahaara before…nightfall."

Her unspoken concern lingered between them. She knew what new surroundings did to him at night. "I will leave early morning tomorrow."

"Another night you will just forego sleep then?"

So she was aware that he had taken to skipping sleep for days together. He stayed silent, refusing to be baited into an argument.

The silence stretched between them.

"Was there a reason you *summoned* me here, Prince Ayaan? More interrogation about—"

He grabbed her arm and turned her toward him. "I never want him mentioned again, Princess, *ever*," he said, enunciating his words through gritted teeth. "Is that clear?"

She nodded, surprising him again. She was definitely acting strangely tonight and he didn't have to think too much to figure out why. "Why do you do that?" he said, fighting the flare of anger at her actions.

"Do what?"

"Call me *Prince Ayaan*? Address me as if we were…"

She quirked an eyebrow, the stubborn jut of her chin more pronounced.

"As if you were a stranger who hasn't seen me at my worst, as if you are not the one person who sees past the prince to the co—" She halted his words with her finger on his mouth, shaking her head. He pulled it away, accepting the very fact he had been fighting for three weeks. "As if you were a lowly servant instead of my wife, my equal."

Her eyes went wide, her mouth trembled. And his curiosity about her multiplied. *Why did she look so surprised?* "And I didn't realize I needed a reason to see my own wife," he said, uneasy with her uncharacteristic silence.

His gaze fell on her hair, and instantly the long, silky length of it draped over his pillow flashed in his mind. It was an image that teased him constantly. "Do I need one to tell her that she looks striking?"

She blinked, color seeping under her skin. She didn't smile though and he wanted to be the one who put it there. For one evening, he wanted to pretend that there was nothing wrong in his life.

He picked up the thin envelope he had left on the table and handed it to her.

She looked at his hand as if he had sprouted claws.

"My mother reminded me of another custom I didn't keep. The groom's gift to the bride."

She looked up at him, her gaze softening. "You spoke to her?"

He cleared the knot of emotion from his throat and nodded. "Mostly she did. But I said a few words, too."

A quiet joy lit up her eyes, her mouth curving into a wide smile. "That's…wonderful. She must have been ecstatic."

She grasped his hands with hers, and a longing of the

most intense kind swirled into life inside him. His gaze stayed on their hands, his throat dry.

She looked down at their hands and stilled. The tension around them could have detonated with the smallest spark. She slowly pulled her hands back as though afraid of just that, but he felt the tremor that went through her.

He leaned back against the wall, and after a second's pause, she did the same at his side. "You like her," he said, surprised. "Even with all the rituals she makes you go through."

She stretched her arms across the wall, a thoughtful expression on her face. The movement stretched the white shirt tight across her breasts and he looked away guiltily. "It's hard not to like her. She is so…strong. She bears so many responsibilities, she has been through so much and yet, through it all…" She cleared her throat. "She's your father's strength too, isn't she? She doesn't let him rule over her. With her by his side, I'm not surprised he was able to weather everything he has with such dignity."

Ayaan had always thought of his father as the strong one. Not that he thought his mother weak. To Ayaan, she was a woman, a mother and nothing more. And yet no one would have been able to stay standing after what had happened five years ago, but his father had kept going.

Because he'd had his wife. And he had taken on immense pain by lying to her. Zohra might not understand it but Ayaan understood why his father had done it.

When you had something or someone so precious, you had to protect her from any pain. In a different reality, he…

He quashed the thought before it could take form. *This night, these stolen moments with her, this was his reality.*

Even this was wrong. But for one night, he didn't want to be honorable.

He wanted to be just Ayaan. Not the son of grieving parents, not a shadow left behind of a beloved brother, not the wrong man to have survived, not the crown prince who was choking under the joy of his people.

He pulled up her hand and placed the envelope in her palm. "This is more of a thank-you than a ritualistic gift."

She took it with trembling hands, the envelope slipping from her grip. He held her fingers in a steadying grip and heard the slight catch in her breath. His own breathing balled up in his throat. She turned it over and over in her hands.

"After a few unsuccessful ideas, I called Saira," he said, to puncture the seductive allure of the silence, to fight the intimacy the evening weaved upon them. "Luckily, she informed me you had no love for jewelry before I settled on a behemoth rock."

Whatever lingered on her lips never found a voice. She opened the seal and the small slip of paper fluttered in her hands. She scanned it quickly, a frown knotting her brows. "What is this?"

"Your itinerary. Saira told me how much you'd always wanted to see Monaco."

Shock widened her beautiful eyes. "My father refused to let me go and I didn't have enough money to go on my own."

"Maybe he was worried you wouldn't come back." Suddenly, he couldn't imagine this world, *his world,* without her. Unease skittered up his spine.

"I turned eighteen six years ago and I have American citizenship. I have a little money to my name and an uncle who lives in Boston. If I had truly wanted to leave, I think I would have left by now." She frowned, as if realizing the import of her own words.

"So...." she swallowed visibly, "this is a trip to Monaco?"

A thread of hope whispered in those words. Utter satisfaction swept through him.

"In ten days, I am heading into the desert for the annual tribal conference." He spoke the words almost without choking. That in itself was a victory. "You can leave for Monaco that same day in a private jet. A family friend will greet you there and take you to the resort we own. My parents have been informed. You will have a security detail. You have a week to yourself, Princess. Without obligations, duties or anything royalty related. The only condition—"

"I won't bring shame upon Dahaar," she whispered.

He turned her around, something in her tone tugging at him. She didn't sound happy, or surprised. She sounded utterly crushed. "I know that it's not exactly the lifetime of freedom that you want, but—"

She moved closer to him, and placed her finger on his mouth. The simple touch pinged along his nerve endings, making him aware of every inch of his own skin. "It's the most thoughtful gift anyone's ever given me."

Her gaze shone with unshed tears, more beautiful than the precious gems he had perused last week. He clasped her face with his hands. "They why do you have tears in your eyes, Princess?"

She clasped his wrists, and smiled through the tears. It was filled with such bleakness, such heart-wrenching desolation that his heart constricted. He waited for an answer that never came.

He could handle the Zohra that was all fire and attitude but this…this hurting, vulnerable Zohra, this he couldn't handle. He couldn't bear to be near because he couldn't *not* touch, *not* comfort. And the comfort he wanted to offer took only one form.

It shook him from within, this need to taste her mouth, to crush her against him.

He backed up against the wall just as she turned toward him, testing his will to the last frayed edge. Before he could blink, she was standing close, too close. He could see himself in her eyes, could see the blue shadows under them and worst of all, he could see the ache in her eyes. Her hands found purchase in his. Her body tilted forward and he was incapable of moving away.

He swallowed, assaulted by an avalanche of sensations and desires. The scent of her bound him to her effortlessly, the whisper of her body's heat sparking an inferno in his. He closed his eyes, willing himself to do the right thing.

She rose up on tiptoes, curled her hands on his chest and kissed him on his cheek.

The touch of her soft lips, the accompanying murmur of *thank you*, the brush of her body against his, and he became unraveled. It was a moment he wouldn't forget in ten lifetimes; a sensation that seeped into his very cells.

The hunger he had been denying himself roared into life with a vengeance. He gripped her nape with his fingers, dragged her against his body and found her mouth with his.

Sparks of pleasure ignited inside him.

Her mouth was so soft, her shocked gasp lost in the friction between their lips. He licked her lower lip and it went straight to his groin. His blood roared in his ears.

He deepened the kiss, forcing her to open up to him and she did. Her surprise lasted maybe two seconds and then she was kissing him back with the same frayed edge of need.

She tasted like everything he had imagined, like sunshine and light, like an oasis in the desert. He worshipped her mouth with his own, his hunger for more burning through him like a wildfire. The graze of her breasts against his chest shredded the last edge of his control.

Grasping her by the waist, he tugged her up until not even a whisper of air could come between their bodies, until every inch of him was trembling, feverish with the need to possess, to consume, to...

He filed away every little sound she made, filed away the feel of her body trembling with pleasure, filed the erotic hunger that swept through him as he stroked her tongue. This taste of her, this feel of her, it had to be enough to root his sanity in ten days.

Zohra felt dizzy with the powerful sensations flooding through her. It was a scorching heat that threatened to turn her inside out, an aching need that began pulsing between her legs.

The taste of Ayaan exploded in her mouth, her whole world reduced to him.

The ground felt like it had been stolen from under her. Her hands laced together around his neck, and she realized she was off the ground.

The assault of his mouth was relentless, stealing her breath and infusing it with his own. Pleasure and pain fused together, rippled out of her in a guttural sound as he tugged her lower lip with his teeth.

His hands around her waist loosened, moved up and down over her back. A string of Arabic fell from his mouth and she realized he wanted to soothe her.

Except she didn't want to be soothed. She wanted to be ravaged, she wanted to forget her own mind, she wanted to...she burned with escalating need everywhere he touched her.

In return, she sank her fingers into his hair, and pressed herself closer, angling her mouth, giving him everything he wanted and more.

One hand at her back pressed her hard against him, one at her nape so that she didn't move, every hard muscle, every ridge and hollow of his body imprinted itself over her, branding her. The hard ridge of his erection rubbed against her belly and a lick of sinful heat bloomed low within her.

His groan surrounded them when she moved restlessly.

His lips learned every inch of her, deep, languorous strokes on one breath, biting and sucking the next. Reverent one minute, passionate and possessive the next. Just when she thought she would expire from the sinful heat his kiss evoked, his mouth left hers and moved toward her jaw.

His hands traveled feverishly over her waist, her back, her name falling from his lips.

She shivered uncontrollably. Her heart pounded, every beat of it a whispered warning.

She wanted to let him fill the hole she had found in her life yesterday. She had already been feeling vulnerable after what Karim had said, and what Ayaan had made her face about Faisal.

But it was Ayaan's gift that crystallized everything for her. This was what her future was going to be—dream holidays with no one by her side.

This loneliness, it was going to be there forever, shriveling her from the inside out. Her future stretched out endlessly with no lasting attachments, no purpose.

The need to find comfort in his arms, to lose herself in his touch, it scraped her raw. She was no more real to him than she was to anyone in her life. But she didn't want to care. She wanted to use him just as he was using her.

She kissed him back with every pent-up longing inside her. Tugging her mouth away from his, she ran her hands over his chest, feeling the solid, hard muscles tighten painfully at her touch.

His mouth found the pulse at the base of her neck. She threw her head back and groaned when he nipped the skin with his teeth. He traced the spot with his thumb, licked it with his tongue.

His fingers moved over her neck, to the slight opening of her shirt. His tongue laved at her lower lip again, and his hand covered her breast, the tips of his fingers splayed against the shape.

She jerked, a pang of delicious need shooting down between her legs.

He didn't move his hand farther, his harsh breaths the only sounds around them. His lips caressed her neck, breathing words into her very cells. "You are turning me inside out, Zohra."

Her name on his mouth, the ragged edge of need in it was an intimate caress, a crack in the fortress around him.

She clasped her fingers around his wrist, and held his palm over her breast, needing the pleasure only he could give. She pushed herself into his touch, shuddering as the tip of his finger grazed her taut nipple. Need knotted there.

His hand tightened over her breast and she moaned.

Before she could draw a much-needed breath, she felt the air around her turn chilly, felt the sharp sting of his retreat.

His cheekbones were flushed with color under the olive skin, his eyes hazy with desire. His chest rose and fell with each breath. His fingers held her with a hard grip. The first sign that not every aspect of him was under control.

Except, he released her and stepped back. Her gut tensed.

She moved closer to him again, every sense alive, as though waking from a long slumber. "Don't call it a mistake."

He didn't. The bleakness in his gaze, the tension simmering around him said it all. "I should not have stayed back or asked to see you." He ran a hand through his hair, palpable rage vibrating beneath his jerky movements. "It will not happen again."

"I have never met another man who detested himself more for what he is, for possessing the smallest weakness. Despite your best efforts, you are a man, not God. There is a limit to how much you can rise above a man's needs and desires."

"*God...Zohra? I am barely even a man.*"

"*By whose standards?* Will you forever measure yourself against your brother?"

A muscle tightened in his jaw, his gaze flashing absolute fury. "Don't. You. Dare. Mention. Him."

Zohra backed down. She couldn't bear to see the anguish in his expression. She took his fist in her hands, unclenching his long fingers one by one.

Ayaan closed his eyes, unable to think with her hand in his. Her skin was soft against his, her fingers trembling. He shivered, every cell in him hungering for her, to touch and shape every rise and dip of her body, to give in to what both of them wanted. Would she be that soft everywhere? Would she welcome his touch everywhere as eagerly as she had enjoyed his kiss? Would she be shocked at all the ways he thought of having her?

"You like being near me, you like touching me," she said, the boldness she sought not hiding the little shiver spewing into her words. "That's why you are here. You made a conscious decision, didn't you, Ayaan?"

He drew a ragged breath in, realized why she had never uttered his name. His name on her lips sounded like an intimate caress that crossed an invisible boundary that neither of them had wanted to breach.

"Tonight you decided to indulge yourself. But tomorrow you will despise yourself for taking this moment. You can't even bear to look at me."

He snatched his hand back, shock robbing him of speech. Every word she said could have been plucked out of his mind. Almost as though she had a direct line to his thoughts.

Self-loathing pounded through him in waves, but not enough to hide the sharp pulse of fear beneath. He had thought to enjoy an hour in her company. But the truth of his hunger for her was far more lethal.

She had somehow become his only way out of a crushing isolation, the one person he sought out instead of running away from, the one person who made him crave normal things even as she brought his darkest fears to the surface.

"If you are saying I came here planning to kiss you—"

"You didn't but it happened. You find comfort near me." She shrugged, reducing his earth-shattering need for her into something inconsequential. "I don't even care that it has nothing to do with me."

How could she be so alluring and frustrating at the same time, so damn perceptive and thickheaded that he wanted to shake her? He fisted his hands at his sides. He would not touch her again. He had done enough harm. "You think the fact that I am drawn to you has nothing to do with you?"

"I'm beginning to see what a clever, cunning man my father is, beginning to understand what Karim meant," she said, shaking her head. "If you were a different man, one not plagued by the atrocities you had to endure, you wouldn't have looked at me, much less married me. But like you said, reality is better if one accepts it. I am beginning to see how miserable I have made myself by not doing that.

"I have been alone for eleven years. I have no friends,

no one to lean on, no one to tell me that I am ruining my own happiness."

She was thinking of the man she had loved and there was nothing he could do to stop it. She moved toward him again and he braced himself. As if she were a knife that could tear into his flesh, a bullet that could lodge under his muscle.

When had this slip of a woman gained so much power over him? How?

She met his gaze, a quiet strength emanating from the very way she held herself. "I have no strength left anymore to be alone, to beat my head against things I cannot change."

He felt spine-tingling cold. There was no other word for the chill that suddenly permeated him inside out. "Zohra... don't."

"I can't go back to Siyaad as a cast-off wife. I can't spend the rest of my life among those people...not even for Wasim and Saira. Neither can I turn my back on them. Which means...this life with you is the only option left to me. And I am not going to fight it anymore."

"You have chosen a hell of a time to stop fighting your fate. Except nothing has changed here," he said, jabbing his temple.

Her gaze was unrelentingly stubborn. The knot in his gut tightened another notch. "I have seen what you think is your weakness and I have not run away. You do not see me as someone tainted. Isn't that enough of a start?"

Anger roiled through him, turning his very blood into bitter poison. "You want to be my wife and play happy family? You want to lie down next to me at night when I devolve into nothing but an animal scared of its own shadow? You want to bear the children of a man who is a disgrace on the very name of his ancestors?"

He hated her at that moment, hated that she was not a traditional kind of woman who wouldn't have dared question his actions, hated that she was a constant reminder of everything he couldn't have, hated that she dared to call him out on his weakness.

"Do you want to strip the last thread of dignity from me?" he shouted, his throat hoarse.

She pushed at his chest, her lithe form shaking from head to toe. Even in her studied indifference toward their relationship, she had been temptation personified. Now she felt like a powerful sandstorm that could bury him beneath the weight of his own needs and desires.

"Is your dignity more precious than living your life? I'm not talking about love and rainbows, Ayaan. In this life, I know that there is no place for anything but duty. And I'm making my peace with that. You came to my rescue, you promised to ruin Karim for what he said to me today. Why can't I—"

His blood still boiled with remembered rage. "You are my wife. Your honor is my honor. I will ruin any man who looks at you wrong, who dares to insult you."

"Can't you see how unique that very statement is in my life? No one has ever looked at me the way you do, as someone worthy of honor, of respect. You are entitled to all that and I'm not? If I can be of help to you, if I can—"

"You think you can save me? That all it takes is for me to open myself to you, to lose myself in your body and I will magically be a whole man?"

"You are a ticking bomb. You barely sleep, you are killing yourself with that physical regimen, you work hours that no sane man does. If you find a minute's comfort in being with me, in…touching me, I am…"

"You will let me into your bed knowing that I'm just using you?" he asked, making his words as insulting and mocking as he could, falling lower than the scum who had insulted her, "Knowing that you won't mean anything more than a willing body to me, knowing that I will never love you?"

She met his gaze unflinchingly, the resolve in her eyes unbroken. "I don't care. I want to have a purpose to my life. I want to...belong in Dahaar."

He shivered where he stood, ice-cold fingers clamped around his spine. "Forgive me, Princess. But I am not one of the projects you take up to fix."

"Then don't touch me ever again. I mean it, Ayaan. No rituals, no gifts, no gestures for the sake of the damned public, I don't even want to breathe the same air as you."

He moved closer to her and she stilled, as if she was gathering herself into a tight ball so that not even his shadow touched her.

Desire was a deafening drumbeat in his very veins.

Had she any idea how much she had worsened his torment by making that offer, how much he wanted to let go of the little honor he had and possess her? How every cell in him wanted a taste of the escape she offered, how much he wanted to steal a moment's pleasure, seek a moment's peace with her?

Because that's what her presence gave him. An irresistible combination of pleasure and peace, except it came with a very high price.

"All or nothing, Zohra? And if I don't agree? If I continue to touch you and kiss you whenever I want without agreeing to your ridiculous proposal?" And he wanted to. He wanted to take the little he needed without guilt cloying him, without regret scouring him. "We both know all it takes is for us to lay eyes on each other to feel it."

"But you won't, will you? You're furious that I dared change the rules on you." A lone tear trailed down one cheek and she wiped it away roughly. "I might know nothing about traditions and customs. But I know a little about honorable men, about men bound by duty, men like my father and you." Bitterness poured out of every word she uttered. "You would rather see the people around you suffer than violate your esteemed principles. You will no more let yourself touch me again than you will realize that you are so much more than the memory of a man long gone."

CHAPTER EIGHT

AYAAN STARTLED, WIDE-AWAKE, sweat beading on his forehead, the bed sheets tangled around his legs. He pulled on his sweatpants and walked to the veranda of his new suite.

The sky was gray, with dawn's first light still a little while away. But he could see the hubbub of activity that had begun near the helipad in the grounds behind the palace. The cold air chafed his bare chest and face, settling deep into his pores. But he couldn't move.

Ground lights illuminated the path, while the lights of buggies used to transport luggage lit the path to the helipad.

One week, all he had to do was to spend one week in the clutches of the desert, in the very place where they had been attacked, where he had seen his brother and sister fall.

Fear fisted his stomach with cold, hard fingers, choking his breath. He gripped the metal balustrade with tight knuckles, reminding himself to breathe through it. It was just his mind playing tricks on him.

But nothing helped. Instead of fighting it, he gave in to the shivers quaking through him and slid to the ground.

He was the crown prince of Dahaar, second son of King Malik Aslam Al-Sharif, a descendant of the Al-Sharifs who had ruled over Dahaar and the desert for ten centuries. Their history was rich, violent, immersed with stories of men who had conquered the desert in all its harsh glory, who had found a way to survive in its unforgiving climate and created a livelihood for their families and tribes.

And he, Ayaan bin Riyaaz Al-Sharif quaked with fear at the thought of a journey into the desert. Shame pounded through his blood.

The conference hadn't happened in six years. One more year would not matter, his father had said, concern softening his shrewd eyes.

And Ayaan had indulged the idea, had felt relief at the temporary reprieve. Until he had seen the one woman whose very presence reminded him of every weakness he couldn't defeat, taunted him with the offer he couldn't accept.

Zohra.

Neither could he wipe the memory of how she tasted. She was a madness in his blood, rivaling the one in his mind.

How many things would he put off, how many duties would he postpone because he feared he was not enough, because he was afraid of what might push him that last step into the darkness waiting for him? He couldn't stand it anymore. He had to know, he had to try, even if he fell over the cliff. He had lost everything in the desert, he had lost himself, but he couldn't let it take any more from him. When he looked at Zohra next, he wanted to have the knowledge of at least having tried, even if he failed.

Or history might as well erase his name from the majestic Al-Sharif dynasty.

Zohra hugged herself tight, shifting from one foot to the other. Her long-sleeved tunic and leggings underneath would be too warm in the desert sun, but even with the pashmina she had wrapped around herself, it was not enough for the early morning chill.

She blinked as the wind buffeted her from both sides. The idea of spending a week in the desert, amid strangers with only Ayaan for company was enough to turn her inside out.

But she couldn't just wait around, wondering if she would ever be able to break from this life, wondering if she would ever have something reaching normal. So she had contacted her old organization and taken on a new project. Meeting the tribal chiefs of Dahaar was an opportunity she couldn't pass up. Not even for Monaco.

"What are you doing here?"

She steeled her spine and turned. The guards and the maids waiting behind them watched Ayaan and her with a hungry curiosity that was becoming the norm.

His face a study in cold fury, Ayaan stood a few feet from her. The frost in his eyes could cut through her skin given half the chance.

"I'm waiting," she said, aware of the tremor in her voice. "Just as you are, for the captain to say that it's okay to board."

His hand clamped over her arm, his scowl fierce. She could feel every ridge, every groove of his fingers, heard the fracture in his harsh breathing. Her belly dipped and dived, the memory of how his mouth had devoured hers seared through her.

"Into the tent. Now, Zohra," he said, flicking his head at a small tent nearby.

Zohra followed him, glad that one of them was keeping an eye on propriety.

All of Dahaar was greedy for every little detail about him. His country loved him but it was also waiting with bated breath, wondering if he would lose it, wondering if their prince would descend into that pit of darkness from which he had risen.

Because even with the strictest confidentiality enforced in the palace, it was clear that their prince was spiraling, toward what no one knew. He worked at a ruthless pace that left normal, healthy people dropping in exhaustion, he was extremely rude to anyone who dared defy him, his relationship with his parents was strained.

He was like a wounded animal that was raring to maim and hurt anyone who dared come close.

Not that anyone could question his sanity or his decisions regarding Dahaar. Not after the past ten days where he had spent countless hours in negotiation with the Sheikh of Zuran building a strategy to counter the terrorist groups that were a threat to all three nations of Dahaar, Zuran and Siyaad. The same groups that had tortured him, that had killed his brother and sister. Not after two terrorist cells had been taken down in one month under his strategic planning.

The media had declared that he was a better statesman than his father was and speculated about the leaps of progress that Dahaar would make under his rule.

If he survived the year...

And standing on the sidelines, watching him push himself without interfering, Zohra had never felt more powerless, more useless.

The moment she entered the tent, he reached her. After ten days of keeping her distance, Zohra was starved for the sight of him.

"Believe me when I say this, Zohra. I have zero patience today. Now, why are you not on your way to Monaco?"

Zohra frowned. Tension radiated from him, the skin tugged tight over his lean features. "I decided to holiday later. Right now, I'm coming with you to the desert for the tribal conference."

"I know how much you have embraced your duty, Princess," he said, sarcasm dripping from his tone, "but let me tell you the truth. No one truly cares whether you are present or not."

His words cut to the weakest part of her. "True, but without me who will dare to tell you that the veneer of civilization is slipping, Your Arrogant Highness?"

"This is the first conference with our tribes in six years." His tone gentled, his gaze lingering over her in an almost pacifying way, the intense hunger in it belying his casual words. "If you are there, your safety will weigh on me."

She had never felt so aware of another person, so clued in to every nuance in a word they said, every gesture they made. She wanted to shake him and comfort him at the same time. "I'm not a stranger to desert life. I used to run a project in Siyaad that—"

"I know about your Awareness Projects, Zohra. You travel to the desert in teams and educate the tribes about basics—hygiene, disease, education, women's health."

"Then are you going back on your word and forbidding me from continuing my work, my life as before?"

He leaned close and her skin snapped to life. The faint scar on the top of his left eyebrow should have made him look flawed. Even just a little would have been fair. Instead, it only added to his powerful personality. "You would like that, wouldn't you? I think nothing would make you happier than if I became that arrogant bastard you envisaged that first night in Siyaad."

She swallowed past the knot in her throat. "If you turned into an arrogant jerk, and by the way you are halfway there, I wouldn't have to worry about you killing yourself.

I would be the merriest widow in the world, wouldn't I? All the freedom and none of the duties."

His mouth touched the corner of hers, and her knees wobbled. Molten heat prickled along her skin even as she cursed her betraying body. "Is Faisal going to be there, Zohra?" He whispered the words into her skin—an assault on her senses and a cutting insult all wrapped in one. "Is that why you are so eager to return to work?"

She pushed his hand from her, tears gathering in her eyes. "You think I proposed starting a life with you ten days ago and now am panting to see Faisal again? I guess you really are no different when it comes to what you think about me, are you, Ayaan?"

She turned away from him, hating the fact that he could wound her so easily. His opinions were beginning to matter too much, and yet she had no way to stop it.

Before she could take another step, he pulled her back to him. He held her loosely this time, his thumb catching the tears that threatened to fall. "*Ya Allah*, I'm not worthy of your tears, Zohra." The frost in his gaze thawed, his mouth lost the tightness. He ran a hand through his hair, looked around, as though searching for the right words. His gaze found her again, hungry, intense. "I spoke without thinking. That remark…it has nothing to do with you and everything to do with me. Please accept my apology."

The air left her lungs in a loud whoosh. "Then accept that I'm coming with you, Ayaan. I did nothing to violate our agreement in the past ten days. I stayed far away from you and believe me, it was a miracle in—"

"You exist, Zohra. That is torment enough for me."

Her heart skidded to a halt. His words spoken through gritted teeth were soft, and yet rang with a depth of emotion. The hungry intensity of his gaze was etched into her mind, the naked want in it inched its way around her heart.

He turned around and walked out.

Hugging herself hard, Zohra stared at his back. Familiar resentment flared at his dismissal. She should turn around, she had never ventured where she was not welcome before.

But she had also spent eleven years doing everything she could to prove that she cared nothing for Siyaad. Perversely, her every action had been shaped by the very thing she refused to be dictated by.

Nothing she had done had been because she'd wanted to do it. She had thought she had loved Faisal, that she hadn't fought back against her father's family because she'd never wanted a place among them, now…now she was not sure of anything.

But when it came to the man who had married her… she wanted to stand by him. Not because it was her duty, not because of what it would mean for her future. But because she wanted to.

It was a crystal clear sign in a sea of murky actions motivated by her anger toward her father, by years of hurt that she had nursed into bitterness.

She had no name for what drove her to it, she didn't even understand it.

But whatever demons haunted Ayaan, she would stand by his side while he battled them. For however long she could.

CHAPTER NINE

SITTING AROUND QUIETLY while Ayaan discussed important matters with the sheikhs of eight different tribes, dressed in an elaborate silk gown that weighed a ton, Zohra wondered what she had gotten herself into.

It was her own fault for talking herself into this trip at the last minute and jumping in without learning anything. She didn't wish she hadn't come, just that she had come armed with knowledge. Like why she was sitting on the biggest divan in the tent with her face hidden by a veil, being studiously ignored by everyone in the room.

The four times she had traveled to the desert encampments in Siyaad, she had been one of three women who had worked there. And no one, including Faisal, had known who she was in the beginning.

Which meant the tribal leaders had barely tolerated her and the other women, and only because their project had been authorized and funded by her father.

Everything had been completely different since Ayaan and she had arrived this morning. The fact that the future queen of Dahaar had graced them with her presence, something they had not been expecting, had thrown the tribal leaders into a hubbub of activity. And before she blinked again, the men had disappeared.

A velvet path had been laid out for her to walk on, and

smiling girls dressed in traditional Bedouin clothes had thrown rose petals on it. Her trembling hand in Ayaan's, Zohra had faltered. She had thought she would feel like a fake and yet, for the first time in her life, she was more excited than disinterested. Maybe because beneath all the fanfare, she was still going to do what she had always enjoyed or maybe because of the man standing next to her.

She had thought his anger over her presence would thaw. But instead, it felt as if she was sitting next to a volcano. Any minute, he was going to implode and she had no idea what would rip the shred of control that was holding him together.

From the cursory glance she had taken around her when they had arrived, she knew the tents were on scales of luxury she hadn't seen when she had traveled before. The campsite was designed around an oasis of native ghaf trees. About four Bedouin-style tents made of richly patterned lambs' wool were scattered around.

They had been immediately provided refreshments while women had arrived from the different tribes to welcome her. Within minutes, Ayaan disappeared leaving her under their care. When they had politely inquired if she was ready to listen to their requests, she had been shocked, even though it was what she had come for.

And so she had spent the afternoon, familiarizing herself with the different tribes, making notes herself, which had surprised the women again, given she hadn't delegated the task.

She had barely rested in her tent when she'd been woken up to be readied for the night's feast. Fortunately, her stylist had packed the emerald silk caftan the queen had had custom-designed for Zohra.

She'd let her maid dress her in the traditional way. Her hands and feet were once again decorated with henna, of the temporary kind this time. Her hair was brushed back and decorated with an exquisite gold comb with diamonds in between. Over it came the veil, woven with pure gold that fell to her upper lip.

When she had turned to the tribeswomen to refuse, one of them had smiled shyly, and burst into an Arabic dialect. Loath to remove that smile, Zohra had kept quiet.

Now, around fifteen men and women sat on smaller divans interspersed around them, all turned just a little bit toward the one she was sitting on. Ayaan was walking around greeting them one by one, accepting their gifts and passing them on to the guard standing back.

An elaborate feast was laid out in the center on a low table, the aromas wafting over and tickling Zohra's nostrils.

Then came that musky scent with something else underneath it that meant Ayaan was moving close. Her breath hitched in her throat. Her vision limited, every other sense came alive at his nearness.

Her hands, tucked in her lap, trembled as he came near.

She could pinpoint the exact moment his gaze fell on her, in the way the very air around them charged with tension.

One of the women burst into Arabic just as he neared her, something between a song and a poem, a beautiful melody that filled the space. Her heart hammering in her chest, Zohra fought to stay still as he tugged the edges of the veil and lifted them up to reveal her face.

His face a mask of tension, he lifted her chin, turned toward the room and said, "My bride and your future queen, Crown Princess Zohra Katherine Naasar Al-Sharif."

His voice glided over her skin. She fought against the shiver that threatened to root itself into her very bones. Congratulations, spoken in Arabic, overflowed around them.

She struggled to stay still as he sat down next to her,

the solid musculature of his thigh flushed tight against hers. Keeping a smile in place, she unlocked her hands and turned. "Shouldn't it be me who is furious, Ayaan? After all, you unveiled me like I was a gift."

His mouth was a study in his fight to calm himself. "On the contrary, it is respect that they offer you. The tribal leaders won't look upon your face unless I grant them permission. Just as I wouldn't presume to speak to a sheikh's wife without proper introduction."

"Like we were your prized possessions."

He held a silver tumbler to her mouth, and she realized the whole room was watching them, their own tumblers raised in mirroring actions. "Drink, Zohra."

His command brooked no argument. Zohra took a sip clumsily. Heat spiraling to life between them, the intimacy of the simple action stole her breath. A drop of it lingered at the corner of her mouth. Ayaan swiped at it with a long brown finger. Desire flew hotly in her blood as though he had lit a spark on her skin with that contact. The cool sweet liquid did nothing to dim the heat blossoming inside her veins.

His gaze staying on her, Ayaan took a sip from the same tumbler and a cheer went up around the room.

"At one point in time the tribes were barbaric people, fighting with each other, among themselves for their very survival. In the last century, civilization has taken root but only a little. In this world, women still need protection— whether from other members of the tribe or other tribes or even royalty themselves. It is a mark of respect, of reverence, something that is taken very seriously. And my duty, whether I agree with their principles or even their form of life, is to respect and protect it."

He turned toward her, and Zohra felt the force of his gaze right down to her toes. Triumph glittered in his eyes, turning them into an indescribable golden hue. "Have you had enough of playing at duty, *ya habibati*? Are you ready to admit that this world is not for you?"

A month ago, or even a day ago, she would have agreed with him, would have been intensely frustrated at the very least. She still was, if she was honest with herself. Sitting there like a package to be unwrapped went against every grain of belief she had fought hard to retain in this world.

But she had also seen and heard firsthand what an important role women played in the tribe's hierarchy from her discussion with the women this afternoon. It was not a life she could see herself living, but she understood it.

Maybe it was the man who took the effort to explain it, or maybe she was seeing the same world, the same traditions and customs without prejudiced lenses.

She shook her head, and had the satisfaction of seeing the mockery in his face relent.

"No, I didn't like being unveiled as if I were something incapable of independent thinking, nor do I like being thought of as your possession, even if it is the most respected one. But neither am I ready to run."

"Why agree to it at all?" His gaze rested on her, curious. "The veil, this ceremony, everything. And don't tell me they forced you. You have no reason to indulge these people. I have seen you in action, Zohra. You are every inch the princess when you wish to be. I am surprised you didn't turn up here in jeans and T-shirt just to thumb your nose at it."

"So little faith in your wife, Ayaan? However shall we get through the next half century in each other's company?"

His mouth tightened again. "Do not challenge me. Your actions in the past decade speak for you."

"I did resent it. But then I thought of you…" A blaze of

heat sparked in his eyes immediately, and she hastened to add, "of your mother and father, of everything your family has lost to protect the tribes' way of living, their independence. And I realized, whether or not I added to your family's name and glory, whether or not I ended up as a minor deviation in your family tree, I wanted to do nothing to lessen it. So I gave in. And I am also realizing that it hasn't made my own beliefs any less."

He stared at her without blinking, and she felt a hot flare of satisfaction that she had surprised him. But it didn't last long, because a truth far more chilling than that suddenly clicked into place in her mind.

"That was why your lives had been sacrificed, wasn't it?" she said, her words loaded with a shiver, with pain she couldn't expel.

His answer was to turn into a block of ice next to her.

She clutched his hand and just as she had guessed, it was ice-cold, rigid. "I read about the history of your tribes but until now, I didn't realize. That's why the terrorists captured you and your brother and your sister.

"They wanted control over the tribes, didn't they? They took you from this very place five years ago and held you hostage? That's why you—"

"Yes," came his gritted answer and even now, she was sure it was only to stop her from probing further.

A knot clawed up her throat, and tears stung her eyes. And this time, she couldn't stem them. She didn't even try. "And your father refused?" She posed it as a question but she already knew. In her heart of hearts, she knew what this life was, she thought she had made peace with it ten days ago, accepted it as her reality.

But the truth about Ayaan's capture hit her like an invisible blow. Her chest was so tight it hurt to breathe.

Her father had walked away from her mother and her.

Ayaan's father had gone an extra step in the name of duty. He had refused to negotiate with a terrorist group, instead he had chosen to forfeit his sons' and daughter's lives.

Two had been killed, and one tortured to madness. But he hadn't bent.

She shivered uncontrollably, and Ayaan's hands wrapped around her shoulders, the heat from his embrace almost, but not quite, enough to thaw the chill in her blood.

"My father did his duty, Zohra. And if the same circumstances came to pass again and it was our child, the very same child who would be the product of the life you are so eager for, that was held hostage, I would be forced to do the same, too. I would probably go mad, take that final leap into darkness while doing it, but I would still do it."

His arm pressed into her shoulders, the heat of his body a deceptively safe haven around her. But nothing could have tempered the chill in his eyes, or the cruel smile that played on his lips. "Are you still eager to belong in Dahaar, Princess, to be my wife in every way that matters?"

Ayaan laughed as he stood at the entrance to the abandoned stables about half a mile from the encampment. Five years of neglect showed in the decrepit structure.

From the moment he had stepped onto the desert floor, the structure had mocked him, jeered him, called to him with its very presence. To resist that call, to pretend that it didn't exist, to pretend it wasn't the cause for the very cold that pervaded his bones, filled him with a white-hot fury.

He had not even indulged the idea of sleeping tonight. So he had ventured out and found himself lingering outside Zohra's tent. There was something to the acute disillusionment, the pain in her eyes that had tugged at him even as he had painted the cruelest picture of what life with him would hold for her.

He had wanted to go in, take her in his arms, do what he could to wipe it from her mind. He understood the loneliness that never left her eyes, understood how it leeched out the simplest of joys from one...

Apparently, his mind had more control than he had assumed because he had no idea when he had moved toward the stables.

He stepped over the threshold, the high dome-shaped ceiling giving it a cavernous feeling. It was a long, rectangular interior, giving a direct view of the empty stalls.

More than one lamp had gone out, the light from the remaining feeble ones just enough to prevent the whole area dissolving into utter darkness. He ran his fingers over his nape, feeling the chill in the air seep into his pores. Goose bumps instantly pebbled over his skin. The smell of the horses and the hay, the echoes of the soft whinnying of beasts long gone hit him with the force of a gale. Every hair on his body stood to attention, his core temperature quickly dropping.

Beware of your triggers. When you feel an episode coming, put yourself in a trigger-free zone.

The words of the trauma specialist reverberated through his skull.

He closed his eyes. Fear dug its claws into him, chipping away conscious thought.

He had loved horses and stables once, it had been his lifeblood. He had spent countless nights in the Dahaaran stables hiding from Azeez. That boy was, however, dead.

His legs struggling to keep him upright, he walked the perimeter of the stables.

He knew what was going to happen. And yet he couldn't walk away. If he was damned to have these episodes for the rest of his life, then he would bloody well have them when and as it suited him.

Distress fingered up his spine and knotted at the base of his neck. He curled his fists, focusing on the simple act of breathing in and out. The quiet took on a life of its own, becoming his worst nightmare. It hammered at him, inching its way past every rationale, every shred of sense he threw its way.

He was a twenty-six-year-old man who was skilled in three different martial arts.

But his psyche didn't understand reason, recycling and feeding itself on fears and terrors from five years ago. The unflinching quiet, the smells and sounds of the stable, all of them pushed under his conscious, inciting reactions that had no base in reality.

A frustrated growl escaped his mouth. He slid to his knees, an invisible rope tugging away at him. And then it came.

The sound that drowned his whole body into a mindless chill, that pierced holes in him. Nausea whirled at the base of his throat. He closed his eyes and gave in to the darkness.

He was sitting on the hard floor, his foot bent at an awkward angle. Winds from the desert howled outside.

A soft grunt reached his ears followed by a dragging movement across the floor of the stables.

Ayaan, can you hear me?

The scent of blood mixed with hay filled Ayaan's nostrils. His fingers gripped slender shoulders, his knuckles beginning to hurt from the tight grip. But he couldn't let go, he would never let go of her. He just needed a moment. His shoulder hurt like hell, and a bullet had grazed his head on the left. Blood dribbled thickly into his left eye.

His vision blurred with tears and his own blood, he felt woozy. That dragging sound came again, the sound rippling across his arms. It was a sound that filled him with the fiercest anger. A cold hand gripped his thigh, its grip strong despite the tremors in it.

Ayaan, you have to leave...

*No...*he roared.

That trembling hand tried to pry his grip off the body in his arms. Ayaan held on tighter. He couldn't let go, ever... he had already made a mistake when he had hesitated to fire, he couldn't make another. Bile filled his mouth. He retched to the side, wiped his mouth.

All he needed was a minute. Once his vision cleared, he would get her out of here...

That dragging sound came again, followed by stuttered breathing.

Ayaan, listen to me. It is too late for Amira and me. You have to leave...now.

Nooooooo....

Ayaan screamed again until his throat hurt, until his head felt as if it would burst from the inside, until pain and loathing was all he became. If only he hadn't frozen like that, if only he had moved faster, if only he had blocked the next shot with his body...so many if onlys....

Something landed on his shoulder, jarring his thoughts. With a scream that never left his throat, he surged to his knees and slammed the intruder against the door of a stall.

Adrenaline pounded through him, rage singing in his veins. This time, he would not hesitate.

One chance and he would drag them all to safety. That's all he needed, one chance.

A soft gasp broke through the mist pounding through his head. He reached out and realized the body of the intruder was slender, almost frail. In that second-long fracture in his focus a well-aimed kick landed on his shin.

The curious scent of roses teased at the edge of his mind. He stilled. That scent was wrong. There should only be blood, tears and the stench of his own fear. There shouldn't be…

He opened his eyes and jerked back so hard that he hit the wall with the back of his head. As his head throbbed, he stilled, his chest so painfully tight that he couldn't breathe.

Dressed in dark trousers and a white caftan, Zohra leaned against the wall, her long hair falling onto her chest over one shoulder.

Bile swam up his throat and Ayaan held it off by sheer will. He moved toward her, his movements shaky and slippery. Emotion balled up in his throat, and he had to breathe through it. Fear beat like a tribal drum in his blood as he tugged her gently.

She fell into his arms, and he thought he might be sick again. He traced the pulse at her throat with the pad of his thumb. And exhaled in painful relief.

Exquisite brown eyes slowly fluttered open.

"Zohra, can you hear me?"

"Yes," she said in a low whisper, "and now that you know that I wasn't about to attack you, can you please let go of me?"

With a curse, he loosened his fingers.

She pushed at his shoulders and he let himself fall back onto his haunches, his gut churning with a vicious force. Her fingers around her nape trembling, she leaned back against the wall and closed her eyes.

Her chest rose and fell with her slow, painful breathing.

He could have hurt her so easily… If he hadn't stopped when he had…

Terror pounded through his blood, a vise squeezing his chest. His hands shook, delayed shock pulsing through him from head to toe. "I could have killed you."

Fire erupted in that beautiful gaze. The fear was all gone now and she was pure, ferocious anger. Her small body bristled with the force of her emotion, her chest rising and falling with it.

She raised her hand and even realizing what she intended, Ayaan couldn't move, couldn't stop her. She slapped him hard, the sound of it ringing around them.

Her chin wobbled, tears falling onto her cheeks. "I am beginning to believe you are truly mad." Her voice was as sharp as the sting of the slap she had delivered. "Why else would anyone invite such pain upon themselves? You knew what might happen to you here. The desert, these stables, this is why you have been such…a monster this past week, why you kept everyone away…" She wiped her tears on her sleeve.

"You saw your brother and sister die here. Why walk in here?" She shoved him again, feeble as her energy was. "I want an answer."

In the face of her angry energy, he clasped her gently, a knot in his throat. "If I hid from it, if I pretended that it didn't exist during this trip, it would forever haunt me. I needed to come here, I needed to see what it could do to me." *When I looked at you next, I needed to know that I faced it instead of hiding.*

Shaking her head, she tugged his hand off her. "And if it had pushed you past that edge, if it had robbed—"

He pulled her to him and tucked his face in her hair. "That was a price I was willing to pay." He swallowed hard, the scent of her seeping into his cells. "My life, Zohra. How could you be so stupid as to follow me?"

She pushed him again, tears flowing freely across her face, trying to break free. "And you think you are not fit to be king, that you don't have what it takes? You are a ruthless bastard, Ayaan. You have all the arrogance that is required to rule your blasted country. Now, let go of me."

"No," he said loudly, crushing her with his arms, emotion robbing him of any sense.

She landed across his knees, the air knocked out of her. She fought him every inch of the way, but he didn't give a damn. He kept his grip on her gentle, but letting go of her was a concept he just couldn't grasp in that moment. She pounded her fists into his stomach. He held her shoulders in a tight grip and forced her head down.

As if sensing his intentions, she stilled. She felt soft and warm against his thighs. Combing his fingers through her hair, he checked for any swelling. There was none.

"There's no swelling, Ayaan," she said, wriggling under his hold.

He closed his eyes, fighting the wet heat of tears prickling at the back of his eyes.

With his hand under her shoulders, he dragged her toward him, nothing gentle left in him anymore.

"I told you there is no swelling, Ayaan. I was just disoriented for a few seconds, that's all. I—"

But he was past caring, past honor, past good sense. He moved to his knees, lifted her up and started walking out of the stables.

"Ayaan, put me down," she said squirming against him.

He tightened his hold on her, crushing her against him. *Did she have any idea how delicate she was? Did she not know what a mindless beast he became in the throes of a nightmare, what a chance she had taken with him?* "No."

"Ayaan, please, you are scaring me."

He had to laugh. *She was scared now?* The woman was scared now after putting him through that? "Again and again, I warned you to stay away from me. But you didn't listen. You made a choice, *ya habibati*. That choice has consequences."

He took the path toward his tent and a shudder went through her. "Where are you taking me?"

"To my tent."

"The maid will tend to me. I want a bath and I want to sleep."

"You can do all that in my tent."

"Why?"

"I could have seriously hurt you, Zohra. A few more seconds and I would have…" He pulled a deep breath in. The hard knot in his throat remained, his chest so stiflingly tight that it was a wonder he was able to breathe at all.

"But you didn't, Ayaan." Her fingers feathered over his jaw. "You stopped. Ayaan, please, it was my choice to follow you, mine. This is not your fault. You couldn't know who it was. You were drowning in that memory, you were not yourself. You can't hold yourself—"

"When you should have cowered from me, you didn't." He stepped over the threshold of his tent and dismissed the guards. "I close my eyes and I see you…against the wall. *Ya Allah*…if you…"

He threw her on the bed, shivering from rage. Her face was pale, her brown eyes glittering in the light of the lamps. "I could not let you go through that alone, Ayaan."

"That image will haunt me now, *ya habibati*." He knelt on the edge of the bed, the need to hold her close, the wanting to touch her, kiss her, blending into an unbearable ache. "Only one thing will banish that image."

She shivered again. "What?"

He shook from head to toe. He wanted to fill himself with the scent of her, with the feel of her. He wanted to hear her scream in mindless pleasure, he wanted to see her thrashing, crying as she came apart in his arms, he wanted to reassure himself that she was alive, again and again.

He swept off the bed, and walked to the entrance to

summon a maid for her. Stripping off his sweat-soaked shirt, he threw it. Utter masculine pride filled him as her gaze swept over his chest with a hunger she couldn't hide. "A new image of you, *habibati*, naked and writhing under me, begging me to be inside you, calling my name as you come undone." He smiled, the dark hunger he had held on to so tightly unleashing inside him. "I am going to make you mine tonight, Zohra. And you are going to wish you had never laid eyes on me."

CHAPTER TEN

ZOHRA WOKE SLOWLY, her eyes adjusting to the soft light of the unfamiliar tent. Her limbs felt too heavy to move, as if they were filled with molten honey. Blinking, she pushed her hair out of her eyes and realized it was still damp from the bath Ayaan had ordered for her.

Solar-powered lamps illuminated a tent that was just as luxurious as hers but much larger. Frowning, she moved to get off the high bed and gasped, feeling an echo of pain in her shoulder. She rubbed it just as Ayaan materialized on the side of the bed.

His hair was damp, and he wore nothing but sweatpants. With a sprinkling of chest hair, the lean muscles of his torso beckoned her touch. She fisted her fingers in the sheets.

Just the sight of him in touching distance, in the same bed, weaved an intimacy that tugged at her. His words as he threw her on his bed came pounding back and a tingle swept down her body.

She remembered the maids coming in and pouring hot water into the claw-foot tub. And undressing her and giving her a massage despite Zohra's objections.

The prince's orders, one of them had whispered with a smile.

"Please tell me I did not faint," she said, inwardly curs-

ing herself. She wanted to add nothing more to the burden
of guilt he already carried.

"I think you like falling asleep in bathtubs, *ya habibati*,"
he whispered and she breathed in relief.

He sat in front of her, his face close to hers. And Zohra
had to remind herself to keep breathing. His fingers found
the sore spot on her shoulder. "Here?"

She nodded, the rough texture of his tone a velvet caress. His fingers moved with long, lingering strokes, reducing her body to a mass of sensation. The tang of his
skin burrowed into her blood. More than physical hunger
uncoiling inside.

She touched his chest, felt the shift of hard muscles
under her seeking fingers, pulled herself forward until
she was surrounded by the fortress of his lean body. With
a sigh, she wrapped her hands around him, everything in
her bracing for his rejection.

Instead, his arms came around her and he held her tight.
Her throat locked down, and Zohra squeezed her eyes shut.
It lasted only an infinitesimal moment but his embrace en-
compassed everything he was.

His fingers crawled up her nape, into her hair. She felt
the press of his mouth at her temple, the whoosh of his
breath over her skin. Swallowing her moan, she hid her
face in his shoulder.

"You smell divine, *latifa*."

She had no control over the next thing she did. She
opened her mouth and licked his skin. Warmth billowed in
her lower belly and pooled between her legs. He tasted of
sweat and salt, like a hunger she had never known before.

A tremor racked his lean frame, the race of his heart a
loud boom in her ears. "I want to be inside you so much
that it is a physical ache…" The naked want in his tone
rolled over her skin. She tilted forward and laced her fin-

gers at his nape. "But, *Ya Allah*, Zohra, after everything you have seen, you still want this?" He buried his head in the crook of her shoulder. His mouth was hot and wet against her skin, branding her, his touch possessive, even as he struggled with himself, with honor that was his very blood. "Because if I touch you, I have no will left anymore to stop."

Her stomach dived even at the thought that he might leave.

The image of him with his head in his hands, his features wreathed in pure anguish—it should have sent her running. Instead, for the first time, she felt the weight of the duty he shouldered with pride and grace, understood the honor he found in giving it his all, the struggle he took on every day without a complaint.

Because this was what he was born to do, this was his reality. She ached to be a part of his reality.

She wanted to give him pleasure, she wanted to be the escape he sought, she wanted to be with him because for the first time in as far as she could remember, Zohra felt no struggle, no confusion, but the rightness of this.

"Ayaan..." she sighed, wondering why her heart always had to choose the hardest path, "I am here not because this is something I have been warned not to do, not because it pushes the boundaries, not because I want to lash out at someone. I want this, I need this, *for me*."

She whispered his name again and again over his skin, the beat of his racing heart the only sound she could hear, his lean, hard body the only thing she could touch. She ran her hands all over his chest, loving the ripple and shift of the hard muscles at her lightest touch.

Another curse ripped from his mouth, another shudder racked his powerful body. With his hands in her hair, he tugged her up. His gaze lit with the blaze of a thousand suns, his desire, his demons, his struggle—everything was laid out for her to see.

He stole her breath in that moment and she had no idea how to hold on to it, how to stop from losing herself in him.

He groaned, the sound weighed down with so much regret. "I have asked for it but I have no contraception, Zohra. And I cannot take a risk—"

"I have been on the pill for a long time," she said, a niggling concern rising to the surface.

His gaze glittered with something unsaid, and Zohra wondered if the perfection of the moment was already fractured. "Ayaan, I know what—"

"Shh…" he said, clasping her face in his hands. "You want me as I am, do you not, Zohra?" She nodded, her heart crawling into her throat, the tightrope she was walking between want and something far stronger blurring at the beauty of the man holding her, both inside and out. "And I want you just the way you are."

He pulled her up until their mouths were inches apart. Anticipation coiled in her stomach, her muscles molten. His mouth was warm, soft against hers, his control a strung out live wire around them. His hands were on her hips, as he licked her lower lip.

Sharp coils of pleasure arrowed lower when he nipped it and licked it again. Demanding, owning, possessive, and this time without an ounce of control. He bit her, licked her and stroked her and did it again. And again. Until their breaths mingled, until their mouths fused, until the rasp of his skin was etched into hers.

Breathing was something he granted her every other moment, and Zohra let herself be taken over.

An erotic swipe of his tongue, a quick sweep of his palms down her body, a whisper of sinful promise at her ear in Arabic. Lost in a sea of sensation, Zohra sank her fingers into his hair and tugged. Pushed her body against his and ran her hands feverishly over his back. "Please, Ayaan…" Her voice broke on a needy sob.

His hands moved to her shoulder, over her arms, his gaze hungry and intense. "I have no memory of another woman's body, Zohra, no memory of feeling this kind of hunger, this kind of need to possess." He licked the pulse at her neck, his breath fanning the flames of her own desire higher. "Do you know how much I have wanted to taste your skin, *ya habibati*, how much I have thought about you like this, how I would stand outside your door and try to remember all the reasons I couldn't come inside and take what I wanted?" He sucked the same spot and she melted into his body. "I threw you out of my bedroom but the scent of your skin remained." He brought her hands to his erection and she jolted at the feel of it. The pull between her thighs intensified at the thought of that velvet hardness entering her, moving inside her. "I have been without relief for a month because I couldn't bear to touch myself. Because what I wanted was your hands on me, your mouth on me." Wetness pooled between her thighs at the shocking eroticism of his very thoughts. She palmed his arousal and he jerked out of her grasp, his fingers clamping hers in a tight grip. "No, Zohra." His fingers traced the neckline of her gown, and her skin snapped into life. "You cannot touch me until my ears are echoing with the sound of your moans, until I have kissed every inch of you, until I have licked you between your thighs…"

Her breath balled up in her throat. His mouth moved along her neckline, trailing wet heat along her skin, kissing and tasting, winding her tighter and higher. The ache between her thighs flared stronger and hotter.

She was so lost in what his mouth did, how it hovered over the curve of her breast, how his very breath seeped into her skin that she had no idea when his fingers had tugged the hem of her gown upward and over her head in one smooth movement. A cool breeze greeted her skin, and instinctively, Zohra lifted her hands.

But his gaze remained lower and she followed it. Molten heat spread across every cell, every inch of her. Her panties were of the sheerest cream-colored silk, cut so deep that they barely covered her mound. And they had tiny white stones at the hem that caught the light of the lanterns hanging from the top and glittered.

"I…" Zohra swallowed as he ran a knuckle over the hemline, a fierce rush of wetness drenching her. "My stylist packed my bags," she finished lamely. He laid his palm, big and warm, fingers down, against her mound and Zohra jerked, and arched into his touch. The bundle of nerves at her sex cried for more. His mouth against her temple, he applied the tiniest of pressure with his fingers. And she sobbed, dug her teeth into his shoulder.

"I told them to ready you for me." He swiped his tongue along the seam of her ear. And she shivered. "Also, remind to me thank your stylist."

The roguishness in his tone was just as arousing as his fingers, and Zohra pushed into his touch.

His hands clasping hers, he bared her torso to his sight.

His eyes, darkened like a desert sky at dusk, roved over her breasts. Her nipples tightened into aching buds.

She squeezed her eyes shut. The sound of his breath, harsh and uneven, pinged over her nerves and she felt a hot rush of satisfaction. "My imagination could not do you justice, Zohra. Do you know how many times I have imagined this?"

She felt his fingers on the curve of her breast and moaned, the relentless dull, ache between her thighs turning into a sharp pull. Felt his abrasive fingers cup the weight of her breasts and jerked. Felt the tip of his fingers circle the tight, painful bud and shivered. Felt the wet heat of his mouth at the valley between, heard him draw in a deep breath, almost reverent. And she shook all over, her legs folding under her. But of course he held her up.

His hair-roughened arms wrapped around her waist, keeping her exactly where he wanted her. Her breasts turned heavy and aching, her throat dried, her breath stilted, but he didn't touch the tautened tips, didn't give her what she wanted, teasing, taunting, until a sob crawled up her throat.

She clutched his hand, ready to push herself into his touch. But he gripped her wrist. His breath fanned over her mouth just before he laved her lips again. "Open your eyes, Zohra."

She looked down and saw the blunt square tips of his dark fingers tweak one aching nipple. Jerking at the pleasure that arrowed right to her core, she moaned. "Look at what I am doing to you," he said in a roughened voice that was pure eroticism.

The sight was so compelling that Zohra couldn't close her eyes even if he asked her to.

He pinched the nipple, and her knees came off the bed. His arm around her waist locked her in place as he bent and sucked the nipple into his mouth.

His name was a cry on her lips that reverberated around the tent, probably in the desert itself. Sinking her hands into his thick hair, she held him in place—a shameless request, a raw command, all rolled into one.

And he suckled deeper, longer, until all she could feel, could see, could hear was the raw strokes of his tongue over the hard tip. Pleasure drenched every cell, every thought on him, every inch of skin quivering with need.

He pushed her back onto the bed with his weight and

Zohra folded, as if her limbs were nothing but sensation. He kissed her navel and downward, and she came off the bed. With a silky, golden-hued scarf, he gently tied her wrists before she could understand his intent. With a kiss on her mouth, he put some pillows under her head. "So that you can see what I am doing to you," he whispered.

Heat unlike anything she had known scoured through her as he trailed wet, hot kisses over the hem of her thong. Then he pressed his mouth against her mound, drew a shuddering breath in. The sheer fabric was no barrier to the sensations that grew within her.

And then he was tugging them off her unresisting legs, spreading them wide, and leaning over her. "Look at me, Zohra," he said, in a voice so heavy with desire, so laden with pleasure that it echoed through her.

Zohra met his gaze and forgot to breathe. She fought against the ties at her wrists, the need to touch him, the need to return the pleasure a dark craving inside her. His fingers were featherlight on her inner thighs, his gaze lust-soaked, primitive, that of a conquering warrior.

And then she felt his breath on the most sensitive part of her and he swiped at the throbbing flesh of her clitoris with his tongue.

Zohra bucked off the bed, shaking, the pleasure that spread through her so acute, so addictive that her hips moved on their own. She cried aloud when he took another long, leisurely lick. A kiss came next, the image of his lush mouth against that quivering bundle shockingly intimate in her mind. He did it again and again and tight coils of sensation gripped her lower belly.

She made sounds—sometimes a sob, sometimes a moan, sometimes his name, begging, whimpering, her head thrashing against the bed, her throat dry. Spiraling need pulled at her, pushed her out of her skin, building when he was there, fragmenting in the infinitesimal moments his touch retreated.

And then he sucked at her core.

Her orgasm rocked through her with the force of a sandstorm. She gasped for breath, the sound spilling from her mouth was erotic to her own ears. Waves of pleasure—acute, breath-robbing—drenched her inside and out. And yet he didn't stop. His hands locking her hips, he continued stroking her with his tongue until he wrung every ounce of pleasure from her body, until she was nothing but a mass of quivering sensations.

The aftershocks of her climax still tumbling through her body, she fell back against the bed. A shiver climbed up from the base of her spine and this time it arose from something inside her, something that wouldn't settle down, something that asked questions she couldn't answer. Keeping her tied hands above her, she moved to her side, a strange shyness coming over her.

His face a dark shadow in front of hers, Ayaan pushed the damp hair from her forehead and kissed her temple. His palm moved over the curve of her hip, over her shaking legs, over her back. The way he cocooned her soothed something inside her that shouldn't have needed soothing. "Zohra?"

Her name on his tongue nestling deep into her, Zohra heard the unasked question and gave an answering nod.

Unwilling to look into the strange feeling, she pushed her bound wrists toward him.

He shook his head, pure masculine arrogance brimming in the golden brown depths. "I have never seen anything so erotic as you coming." His fingers traced the curve of her butt, drew maddening lines up and down her spine. "I think I might get addicted to it."

When he touched his mouth to hers, she moved her

head, although not before the taste of him seeped into her lips. "I think the entire encampment heard me, Ayaan," she said, her lust-soaked body catching up to the niggling warning from her mind. "Is it—"

"Nowhere near enough, *ya habibati*," he said, grasping her question without being asked. Pushing her back into the bed, his body settled on top of hers. The hair on his legs rasped against her, the angular contours of his hips an intimate caress. He felt heavenly on top of her, the heavy weight of him a pleasure that rendered her mute.

"Ayaan?"

His face buried in her nape, he smiled. "Hmm…?"

"I…" the words she wanted to say rose to her lips and fell away. Fear was a tight knot in her throat. This moment with every inch of him flush against her, the ever-present shadows in his eyes at least held back for now, she didn't want to fracture its fragility, she didn't want to risk another's name entering it.

She arched as he sucked at her neck, and then licked it. "I want something from you."

His grip on her hips tightened an infinitesimal bit. "Tonight, anything you want, *ya habibati*."

"I have dreamed of touching your scar, of kissing it, of tracing it with my tongue."

She felt the rush of his exhale between her breasts. In the next second, her wrists were unbound. And he fell back against the bed.

She took in the sight of him, her breathing, raspy, shallow.

His hair falling onto his forehead, his arms resting above his head, the contours of his chest narrowing to his waist, the hard, tight abdomen, lean hips covered by the sweatpants, olive-colored skin gleaming with a sheen of sweat—it was an intimate sight she hugged to herself, a sensual feast that would forever be etched onto her mind.

Staying on her side, she ran tentative fingers over the winding scar, felt the puckered tissue. Tears rose in her throat and she swallowed them down. No, there was no place for sorrow in this moment either. "How did you get it?" she breathed the question into his skin, hiding her face.

The tangy scent of him held her in place, the gentle stroke of his fingers in her hair rooting her to that moment.

"They bound me with a metal rope that had several knots in it."

A matter-of-fact reply.

She caught the sound of horror before it left her mouth. Sliding close, which rubbed her breasts against his side, she pressed her lips to the scar. His hands tightened in her hair, his abdomen bunched so tight that it took her a moment to understand.

He liked it.

Pulling herself up on an elbow, she ran her tongue slowly over the length of it, peppering it with kisses. "Turn around," she said.

And to her delight, he did. With his darkly hungry gaze trained away from her, she was bolder. Sliding to her knees, she kissed it all the way across his torso. Her nipples grazed him again and this time, they both groaned.

"And again," she whispered, and he lay on his chest.

She bent forward to reach the other side, and her hand fluttered over his chest, down to his navel and farther below.

Until her fingers grazed his erection. A hoarse grunt fell from his mouth, his hips thrusting upward into her hand. She palmed it, the rigid, pulsing length of it sending a rush of wetness to her core.

And then, before she could blink, he was on top of her, deliciously heavy.

His gaze collided with hers. Naked desire burned bright with dark shadows that always lingered but something else shimmered in his eyes, something that burrowed into her heart, wound itself around her. "You didn't ask me permission to do that."

A glimmer of contentment, that was what it was.

It was a gift, it burst through her like an explosion, a sight she gripped tight.

He pressed a hard kiss to her mouth, and Zohra felt the tempo of his kiss change. His hands moved over her body, thorough and erotic but now, there was an urgency that shattered that iron-fisted control. When he settled between her thighs and probed her entrance with the head of his erection, every thought disappeared from her head. And Zohra was lost again.

Would it ever be enough?

The unrelenting question pounded through Ayaan, mingling with the desire coursing through his blood, reverberating in every cell.

It had to be, he threw an arrogant answer at himself.

Because this was sex, after all.

Zohra might be nothing like the women he had known, but his body was reveling in the pleasure, in the simple act of touching, of kissing.

Ayaan ran his mouth over the pulse at Zohra's neck, the taste of her tightening the need drumming through him. Her thighs automatically fell away, making a place for him, cradling his erection, the rasp of her quivering thighs against him unraveling the last thread of his control.

She moved under him, a rasping sound from her throat.

Her breasts rubbed against his chest and his arousal tightened into steel.

He licked one taut nipple, and she arched like a bow, her hands sinking into his hair. He pulled it into his mouth and she screamed his name.

It was a needy, throaty sound that ripped through him. "Please Ayaan…" she whispered at his ear, before flicking at his earlobe with her tongue. "I want to touch you, I need to…"

Shaking his head, he ran a finger over the swollen flesh between her legs. She dug her teeth into his shoulder. He plunged a finger into her sex and she bit him, hard.

Ya Allah, she was wet and ready for him. He wanted to pleasure her again, bring her to climax, suffuse himself with the taste and scent of her but the sight of her pink flesh, wet and ready for him, and his own hunger—selfish and relentless, rode him hard.

Pushing her legs wide, he rubbed at the entrance with his penis. Sweat beaded on his forehead, every inch of his body throbbing for possession.

"Spread your legs for me, Zohra," he said, in a voice that was far from his own.

When her boneless legs moved farther apart, he kept his hands on her hips and entered her in one hard thrust.

Stars exploding in his eyes, she clenched him tightly. Heat poured through his muscles, pushing for friction, the walls of her sex stretching around his erection. He was about to pull out and ram back into her when the stillness of her body filtered through to his lust-soaked mind.

He looked into her eyes, and saw the truth reflected there. Shock poured through him. "Of all the things to be lying about, Zohra?" he said, followed by a vicious curse he hadn't ever uttered before.

Regret punctured the pleasure, but only a little. His

thighs quaked at having to stay still. He pulled back, inch by excruciating inch, his shoulders feeling like steel rods at the pressure he put on them to be slow, to be gentle, when she moved the tiniest inch beneath him.

He bent down and nipped her lips, not hard but not gentle either. "Stay still, Zohra," he said through gritted teeth, his skin sweaty, his hair drenched, and his body sliding out of its skin with the need to move.

But of course his willful wife paid no heed. "It doesn't hurt, Ayaan, not anymore. It just feels…" Her hands gripping his shoulders, a thoughtful look on her face, she wiggled her hips upward again. "Ahhh…it feels full and achy and so good…Please, please move…"

Heat spiraled down his spine. With a curse that reverberated around them, he pushed back into her. Her throaty moan scraped along his skin, the experimental thrust of her hips blinding him to anything but sensation.

Pleasure soaked into his skin, rammed through his nerves until there was nothing but the wet heat of Zohra, of his wife. Giving in to his body's natural rhythm, he moved again. There was no finesse to his thrusts, no filter on the words that left his lips. Her thrusts met his in perfect rhythm, the sounds she made became needier, faster. He willed his body to wait for her pleasure by the skin of his teeth.

On the next move, he rubbed the swollen flesh with his fingers and she fell apart like a thunderstorm. Her muscles contracting against the sensitive flesh of his arousal, pulling every inch of pleasure from him, he thrust again and orgasmed in an explosion of heat that touched every nerve, rocked through every inch of him.

Pleasure receded, the first wave of need blunted for now, and questions pounded back into him. He reversed their positions, still joined intimately.

Her arms instantly rose to cover her breasts. She looked down at their bodies still joined and a fierce blush claimed her cheeks.

"You were a virgin."

Her gaze flew to his. "Yes."

He pulled her hands from her breasts, fresh need rippling through him at the sight of those pale pink nipples. She held herself stiff, and the savage that he was, it turned him on. "You said—"

"Let go of my hands, Ayaan."

"No," he said and pulled her up until she was astride him in his lap. His erection thickened, lengthened inside her.

Her brown gaze flared wide. "Oh….you are—"

"Yes, *ya habibi*. It's a long way down from the edge."

The most masculine, arrogant, savage satisfaction gripped him now that the initial anger at her lie faded. He frowned, even as he relished the feral feeling.

Fierce emotions—either passion or fury or even love, he had never been capable of them. And yet in that moment, he couldn't stem the savagery of his emotions.

Questions hurtled through him but he fought the urge. He would not bring another man's name into this bed with her. Not tonight, not ever.

He was the only man to have possessed her, the only one who had known her in the most intimate of ways.

Her hands resting on his shoulders, she tried to wiggle out of his lap. The erotic friction of their joined bodies intensified a thousandfold.

Their mingled groans, the scent of sex—it was an irresistible aphrodisiac.

"You lied to me."

"I said and did whatever I thought I needed to, to get out of the wedding," she said. "But Faisal never asked for what I would have offered. I used to tease him for being so bound to traditions and customs that were laid down ages ago. But I think I understand now. And I..."

He clasped her chin, forcing her to look at him. "Finish your thought, Zohra. Because this is the last time I will tolerate his name on your lips, the thought of him on your mind."

She looked at him, unblinking, the depth of emotion in it a reminder of what a force this woman was. "I am glad he never asked, Ayaan."

He closed his eyes and breathed through the cloud of need that had his hips leaning upward into her. She had been a virgin, he reminded himself with the utmost effort. He needed to be gentle, even if it was a little late, he needed to let her body get used to him. "What does it make me that I am glad that he didn't take it, Zohra? That your body has known only me, that..."

She lifted her hands, sunk them into her hair and tugged it back. It was such an unconsciously sensual movement that he lost that tenuous hold on himself. "Like I felt when you said that you don't remember another woman's body, when you said you never felt pleasure like this before?" He couldn't help himself. He cupped her breasts and rubbed the tight nipples with the heel of his palm. "Whatever you think it makes you, I am one, too. So be kind to yourself," she said, and arched into his touch with a sigh.

He bent his head and licked one nipple. She jerked, moving up and down, and it was his turn to groan. "Your breasts...I am never going to have enough. And you go up in flames when I touch them."

"Yes," she whispered, her spine so straight that he wondered if he would break her. Her lips were swollen from his kisses, the marks from the stubble of his jaw outlined on her neck and breasts. What in the name of God had she unleashed in him? She leaned her forehead against his and the trust in her action branded him. "I...it feels like I will combust..." She arched her body again, as if asking him for more, "...if you stop."

Just once more, he promised himself. He would taste her just once more and then stop. Let her body breathe, let her rest. He pulled the nipple into his mouth and suckled. And she sobbed, his name falling in a guttural request from her lips. He heard his name on her mouth, the whimper of pleasure she made, that shredded his composure.

They were sounds he would never have enough of.

Burying his mouth at her neck, he fought for control. With her hands locked around his nape, she pushed closer to him until her breasts dragged deliciously against his chest. And kissed him on the mouth.

He gripped her hips when she moved, heat he had no strength to check built up inside him again. "You will be sore tomorrow, *ya habibati.*"

Her tongue traced the seam of his lips, her eyes twinkling. His grip loosened on her, his body moving of its own mind. She sucked on his tongue next and he lost the fight.

He thrust upward and she moved down. He pumped his hips faster, and she matched his rhythm. He cursed and she laughed. Leaving her to set the rhythm, he took her nipple in his mouth.

And she shattered with a guttural sigh. His own climax followed, rippling through him, breaking him apart and putting him back together and changing him.

Taking her with him, he fell back to the bed, and held her tight against him.

His memory wasn't that corrupted to think his body had once known this kind of pleasure, his mind not so broken to think what had occurred was normal, to believe that it was anything short of spectacular.

Six years ago, he would have reveled in the discovery, taken it for granted as another of life's gifts, shouted it out from the rooftops. The man he was today couldn't stop the cold ripple of fear that churned in his gut, couldn't shake the feeling that anything this good couldn't last.

CHAPTER ELEVEN

MEET ME AT the stables.

Ayaan looked at the note a little girl had fluttered in his hand. Frowning, he looked up and realized he had missed half of what Imran, his security chief, had said.

Motioning him to repeat, he walked toward the stables. And promptly stopped on the path when Imran was done. "So this information comes from the same source who provided us information last time on where the terrorist group will convene next?"

Imran shook his head. "No."

Intelligence about a terrorist gathering in Dahaara the next month... It was the third time this information was coming his way. Information that had been accurate the first two times but was beginning to sound too good to be true. And this time, it was coming from a different source.

Something niggled at Ayaan, even though he couldn't exactly place it. "See if you can trace it back to the source," he said, taking another step in the direction of the stables.

"Are we not—"

"We are not acting on this until we figure out if there is a connection," he said, dismissing him and covering the distance to the stables.

Imran had requested this meeting two days ago, and Ayaan, unable to focus on anything, had forgotten.

Like a teenager riding the first waves of infatuation, his mind, and his body, refused to focus on anything but on the image of Zohra underneath him, her beautiful brown eyes bewitching with raw need, sparkling with trust, the tight heat of her body, the heady moans from her mouth.

At some point past midnight, when he had exhausted them both, they had finally fallen sleep. Dreamless sleep, Ayaan had realized with a shock the next morning.

It had been two days since, two days where she had occupied his every thought, during which, interestingly, she had avoided him just as he had, where he had had more than enough time to berate himself for what he had done, to find numerous reasons why he could not do it again.

Even if his body, forever in a state of painful arousal, didn't understand the fact.

He made his way to the stables, curiosity for once trumping the distinct unease he felt anywhere near it.

He stood inside, the echo of everything he had gone through in there rumbling through him. He understood the spine-tingling fear that had driven him to take Zohra, the need to keep her close, the need to lose himself in her body, but in the cold light of the day, the evidence of the instability of his mind skewered through him.

The scent of her carried to him through the light breeze, his body thrumming to life as though a switch had been turned on. He turned around to face her and frowned. Dusk was still a few hours away yet she had wrapped a thin shawl over her torso with white leggings under it. Her hair was covered with a scarf of the same color, and she looked the very picture of vitality, of life, an embodiment of everything he was not.

"Ayaan," she said, as if she needed to force him to acknowledge her presence, as if the memory of how she tasted, how her body clenched him tight wasn't etched into his very cells.

"You have been avoiding me," he said. Tugging the scarf from her neck, she dropped it to the floor. Sunlight glinted in her hair, turning it into strands of coppery gold. "Are you regretting what happened?"

"No. And I'm not the one who's doing the avoiding. I just didn't hound you like I usually do." She ventured farther in and tugged the huge door closed. Then her fingers pulled the shawl she had wrapped around her torso. Inch by inch, she unwound the fabric until it fell to the ground with a soft whisper.

She wore a sleeveless top, in the sheerest see-through silk in gold. With the light from the high windows behind her, every inch of her body was outlined under the thin fabric. He swallowed, the shadow of her lacy bra, the indent of her navel instantly drowning him in images and sensations of how she had felt beneath him.

Walking around the stables, she came to a halt near him. "I have ordered for it to be demolished."

He raised a brow even as he enjoyed the raw command in her tone.

Sinking her hands under the top, she slowly peeled off her leggings. The sight of her long, bare, sun-kissed thighs set need coursing through him, rattling his self-control. "It serves no purpose other than to remind you of what you had to endure."

"It's not the only thing that reminds me of everything I have gone through and everything I am not," he said, studying her with a hunger that was becoming all too familiar. The sight of the thin strings of her panties dried up his throat. "And demolishing it won't fix me, Zohra."

Shaking her head, she reached him, a resigned smile on her lips. "Maybe I don't think you need fixing, Ayaan.

There is one thing I wish to do here before it goes down, though."

She was upset and she was battling it with her fierce strength. He didn't question why or how he knew. He just did. And in this mood, she was a force to be reckoned with.

He covered the last step between them before he realized he was moving. Being near her and not touching her was akin to not breathing. Their gazes held, speaking to each other, assessing each other, and he immediately felt surrounded by her warmth.

Warmth that had a different source from the desire that flew hotly in his veins. This time, he willingly lost the fight, surrendered his will to her.

His fingers trembling, he touched her forehead. She exhaled on a whoosh. "Are you all right?" Burying his nose in her hair, he took a deep breath, until she was all he knew, all he felt, all he was. "Everywhere?"

Her chin tilted up, she held his gaze even as pink scoured her cheekbones. "I am not going to break so easily." Her words were a challenge, a gauntlet thrown down. And yet, he could be the one who could break her, who could crush that indomitable spirit.

She ran her fingers over his jaw, and he closed his eyes. Her touch feathered over him, fanning the flames of desire that always simmered. It had taken him an incredible amount of control to not go looking for her in the past two days.

The indescribable pleasure he had found with her was addictive, but he could still do without it. But the warmth of her smile, the quiet contentment he found near her, he was afraid they would be his downfall.

The pads of her thumbs brushed over his forehead, his nose, his lips. When he would have stopped her, she pushed his hands away. "You will not deny me this."

"Giving orders, Princess?"

Her hands moved lower, lingered over his neck. "No, simply exercising my rights as your wife."

She kissed his cheek, tugged at his earlobe with her teeth, scraped them over the pulse in his neck. Her nimble fingers began unbuttoning his cotton shirt. Need gripped his belly, his arousal instantaneous, powerful and relentless.

She pushed him against the wall and he let her, enjoying the daring in her gaze, more than content to see how far she would go.

Pushing his shirt off his shoulders, she kissed his pectoral. "You are like steel covered in velvet. My fingers itch to touch you, to scrape you, to mark you as you did me."

His breath balled up in his throat. "Do it," he said, wondering how easily she enslaved him.

She raked a fingernail over one nipple and he fisted his hands at his sides.

Her hands clasping his on either side, she bent and scraped her teeth over the other nipple. A hiss of breath left him as his skin felt too hot, too tight to hold him. Her pink tongue darting out, she licked him, and his erection twitched.

Like a cat licking up cream, she rained soft, wet kisses over his chest, his abdomen, around his navel. His muscles knotted so tight that it almost hurt, but he resisted the urge to sink his hands in her hair.

She licked a path next to the line of hair disappearing into his jeans, and he bucked off the wall. He closed his eyes, fighting for control. Instead the image of her mouth around his arousal burned in his brain. He felt her fingers undo the button, tug the zipper down.

Heat billowed in his blood, curled in his muscles, threatening to shove him out of his own skin.

He uncurled his fingers and plunged them into her hair. "Stop, Zohra," he said, uncaring that his tone was begging for something even as he spoke the words that said the opposite.

She sank to her knees at his feet, full of fluid grace. She looked up, her eyelids droopy with lust. "Remember how you gave me a gift, Ayaan?"

He nodded, his throat hoarse.

"Apparently, the bride is supposed to give one to the groom, too. The next time you think of this place, I want you to see me like this—on my knees, with my mouth around you."

An unbearable longing churned through him. "You don't have to do this, Zohra."

"I want to. Just as you wanted to learn and taste every inch of me."

With a smile that he would never forget curving those lushly erotic lips, she tugged his jeans and boxers down. And his erection sprang free.

Clamping his jaw tight, he closed his eyes. He heard the harsh rasp of her breathing, just before she wrapped her hand around his hard length, her fingers tightening as they moved up and down.

He instantly jerked his hips forward, coils of pleasure shooting down his groin.

Until he felt the tentative flicker of her tongue over the head. Heat blasted through him.

"Oh…" she said, her breath feathering over the wet tip.

He sucked in a breath, tried to get his vocal glands to work. "What?" It was all he could say.

"I see why you liked doing it so much." Her pink tongue flicked out again and stroked him in a leisurely lick that tugged tight over every nerve ending. "Every time I do that, I feel this ache...." She shifted restlessly on her knees, before licking him again.

He banged his head against the wall, a low growl ripping from this throat when she closed her soft mouth over the head.

"Where?" he rasped again, his brain only capable of single words.

He heard her soft groan in the moment that she caught her breath. "Between my thighs. Every time I taste you, I feel it there," she said, before sucking him into her luscious mouth again. His shoulders trembled, his knees quaked, a fine sheen of sweat covered his entire body.

She continued pleasuring him with her tongue and her mouth until he shook with the sensation of it, until curse upon curse fell from his mouth, until he could feel the intense rush of his climax building, a roaring fire inside him.

Holding on to the last vestige of control, reining the animal part of him that wanted only to find release, he tugged her up.

Her skin was flushed, her gaze soaked with lust. With movements that lacked both finesse and gentleness, he tugged her panties down and lifted her up against the wall. Her legs wound around his hips just as he thrust into her in long, smooth motion.

Pleasure, so acute that it bordered on pain, rode through him.

This time, he didn't stop or think. He gave in to the need pounding upon him, the musky scent of her arousal telling him everything he wanted to know.

His orgasm was a breath away, but he didn't want to ride the wave, not without this amazing woman he had married falling headlong into it with him.

He wanted her to splinter, he wanted to hear his name on her lips, here—in this place of all places—where something inside him had been forever lost, in the one place that stood for everything he was not and that she deserved.

With a voracious need that he now knew would never be satisfied, he pushed her top up until he found bare skin. He tugged the lace of her bra down and found a taut, aching nipple.

He pinched it between his fingers and she came undone. He kissed her mouth, loving his name on it as he pounded into her, their mingled groans and grunts rippling through the air.

Her hands in his hair, her teeth dug into his shoulder, just as he came in a fierce rush of pleasure. She whispered his name just as he wanted and it stole over all the cracked, broken places inside him.

Nothing would fix him, he knew that now, but in the moments when he was with her, Ayaan could almost believe that he was a better man, a man worthy of the amazing woman. Stealing a kiss from her, he righted their clothes and crumpled to the ground.

Leaning against the wall, he pulled her close until she was cradled between his thighs. Wrapping his arms around her, he kissed her shoulder, clutched her to him tight.

The most amazing kind of contentment ballooned up in his chest that he wondered if he would burst from it. "Thank you, Zohra," he whispered, his heart beating loudly, loath to fracture the fragility of the moment.

She nodded. He had no idea how long they sat like that. But as minutes passed, Ayaan felt the tight fist of fear this place held in his core relent. Running his hands over her shoulders, he wrapped his arms around her waist.

"Zohra?"

"He has had another heart attack."

Her words were so soft that he didn't catch them until

he felt her shiver. "I will arrange for your transport within the hour."

"I don't want to go."

She turned suddenly and hugged him hard. Her arms clamped around his neck, her face buried in his chest, Ayaan felt a fierce rush of tenderness swamp him. She was hurting and he understood the feral urge inside of him that wanted to fix everything for her.

"I am scared, Ayaan," she said, breathing the words into his neck.

He frowned at the shiver that spewed into her words. It spoke of a Zohra he had never seen or heard. "You afraid, Zohra? Of what?"

"Of truth, of seeing him, of learning of things that I never let my father say. But I have to ask him this time."

He held her as she steadied herself, as she found her own strength again. "Remember what you said about truth, Princess? That even in its bitterest form, it is better than the sweetest lies. You have evaded it for thirteen years now, have let the very idea of it have power over you. He could have let you go to your uncle, he could have let you go through your entire life thinking he was dead, he could have easily shrugged off your responsibility, he could have placed so many restrictions on how you led your life. But he didn't. It is time to face the truth, Zohra, time to see if it can really break you as much as you fear."

"It didn't break you, Ayaan. Being in this place, living through it, you are still standing."

The very contentment he had felt a moment ago slid off him.

Still standing, that was what he was, that was what every small step he took amounted to in the end. Not that he gained control over his fears, not that he had made a small amount of progress, no.

His victory would always be that he hadn't fallen back into the madness.

Even after he had realized the truth of what had happened to him, he hadn't resented his life, he had accepted his reality without complaints, shrugged on the mantle of duty to the best of his ability.

But the moment he was near her, this crippling need flared inside him—to be more than what he was for her, this emaciating, perverse anger over circumstances he could not change, it gnawed at him.

Wasn't that why he had risked this journey to the desert, risked his lucidity and everything it meant to his parents and Dahaar? Because he wanted to be a better man for her? Wasn't he compromising the one thing he still had, his sense of duty, his honor, in her name?

Zohra burrowed into Ayaan's embrace, even as she felt his cold retreat. Two days—she had held herself back, checked every impulse to go to him before she lost the little headway she had made with him.

The need to bear his pain for him, to help him through it, festered inside her. She couldn't. Instead, she had wanted to dilute it, loosen its hold on him. And she was glad she had tried, she was ecstatic that he had let her, that she had held power over him in that moment, in making the powerful, honorable man that he was sway with need for her.

But that pleasure, she realized now, would always come at the price of losing whatever small connection she found with him.

Because until he realized everything he already was, Ayaan would loathe any pleasure he let himself feel, reject any happiness he found with her.

It was what she found with him, too. Even in his grief, his nightmares, being with him was what made Zohra the most alive. As if she had woken up from under a heavy blanket of resentment, of misplaced anger, of fear.

Even in the short time she had known him, seeing his struggle to rise above what he was, his honor in always doing the right thing, Zohra was finally awake. In a way she had never been until now.

She turned around in the cocoon of his arms, clasped his jaw, took a greedy kiss from him. As if she could bind him to her will by touching him. Because whatever she had from him, it was never enough. And today, she wanted another piece of him, she wanted something he had never given anyone else, she wanted his pain, his suffering. "Will you tell me what happened here?"

She thought he would refuse, shut her out, walk away. His tight grip on her fingers was the only sign that he had even heard her. "I have never spoken of it, to anyone." A smile curved his mouth, bitterness etched into every strong line of his face. "Is this the final test, Zohra? Because if I speak of it, it will forever change how you see me. You will see what I see when I look in the mirror."

"You can't imagine what I see when I see you. Please, Ayaan."

"It was going to be the last time our entire family attended the conference because Amira was to be married in a couple of months. Our parents had already left with most of the guard thinking we were accompanying them. But Amira and I learned that Azeez was staying back and decided to confront him."

"Confront him?"

His breath fanned over her nape, his hold on her tighter. "The three of us, we had always been close. But something had been eating at him for almost a year. He became a different person, not the brother we knew. It hadn't escaped our parents' notice either. His coronation was only months away, and he had been avoiding both Amira and me. So we thought it was the best chance.

"And before I knew it, we were surrounded on all sides by armed men. But the strange thing was that Azeez had been prepared, he surprised them by instantly going on attack. He was something to watch, the way he fought. And we had a good chance of getting out of there, too. I caught the gun that he threw at me, but then a bullet hit Amira and I...I just froze."

If she hadn't felt his chest rise and fall, Zohra would have thought he had turned into ice right in front of her eyes. He raised his hand and looked at it as though he still held the gun. His face puzzled, his mouth held the bitterest of contempt.

And she found no words to say to him that could break through the dark cloud of self-loathing that poured out of his every word.

"I could not raise my hand and shoot. I just couldn't. To this day, I ask myself why not. When he needed me, when my sister needed me, I failed.

"I didn't shoot or even move to cover him. He got shot in the hip, and a bullet grazed my head...but even then, I just stood there, staring at him, useless.

"When I woke up next, Amira's body was next to me while Azeez...he couldn't move."

Zohra wiped her own tears, the deep chasm of grief beneath his monotonous tone ringing through her. She forced herself to ask the next question, even as she never wanted to hear it again. "Did he die in front of you?"

With a smoothness that startled her, he stood up. She saw the tremble in his hands as he pushed his hair back. He paced like a caged tiger, the fury rattling from him a tangible thing in the air. "No. They bound me but not him, because his leg was already useless. Blood...there was so much of his blood everywhere. He kept telling me to try to leave…until suddenly he just lay still and they dragged him out of there. They needed us for negotiation. I remember thinking he would get medical aid, thinking…

"I didn't see him again, have no idea what they put him through.

"I remember every moment of that cursed day until then. I have no idea how long they held me, how I escaped, no idea where they buried him. It's the question I see in my mother's eyes when she looks at me and I don't have an answer. I have racked through my mind, but I…"

"Shhh…" Zohra whispered, hugging him, her own tears beating a path down her cheeks. She was not sorry she had asked. Because this grief was a part of him and she wanted all of him. She only wished she could bear its weight for him, even if for an infinitesimal second.

"Every time I hear the word courage associated with me, I cringe, I fall deeper into the pit of my own shame. Are you disgusted by me now, Zohra?" His words whipped through the air around them, polluting everything they had shared just minutes ago.

She held his face in a tight grip, a lump lodging in her throat.

Her chest was so tight that it was a wonder she could breathe. It hurt to see him hurt, it hurt that she couldn't help him, it hurt that he would never embrace the little happiness he found with her. It hurt so much that her stomach lurched, her breath halted in her throat as an image of her life, forever waiting for him, within reach but far away, stretched in front of her.

He would do his duty by her, stand by her, maybe even create a child with her—because this pull between them was stronger than either of them, but he would never look at her with happiness, never accept her love, never return it.

Fear like she had never known before filled her veins.

How had she fallen in love with a man who was the very epitome of everything that had gone wrong in her life, a man who would give her his name, his honor, his life in the name of duty but not his heart?

And this time, Zohra understood what love meant. She understood that it was not a battle of wills, of individual needs and desires, that it demanded sacrifice, that it demanded everything one had. It flew through her, strengthening her and weakening her, glorifying her and damning her, freeing her and yet forever binding her to him.

She sucked a deep breath in, striving to hide the biggest truth of her life. If he realized even a flicker of what she felt for him, she knew he would banish her from his life. She would lose even the little she had.

"You were twenty-one years old, Ayaan. After all these years, can you not forgive yourself even a little?" she asked, her own sorrow bleeding into her words, "Can you not permit yourself to pursue your own happiness?"

His refusal was impenetrable, sealing her fate right along with his. "Not when it cost them their lives." The darkest of smiles curved his mouth, a cold chill dawning in his gaze. "I think you know me better than I know myself. You knew what you were going to get and you still wanted it, Princess." His mouth found hers in a punishing kiss, every stroke of his tongue a brand of possession, every caress calculated to master. He licked the seam of her ear, and Zohra clutched him swaying on her feet. "Do you want an out now, Zohra?"

She met his gaze, her heart in her throat. "Will you give it to me if I wanted it?"

He lifted her up and carried her out of the stables. "No. I have cast off what little honor I possessed, Zohra. Now you are bound to me forever, damned to this life right along with me."

Lacing her hands around his nape, Zohra hid her face in his chest, an intense sadness weighing her down. Just as he had said, she had entered this relationship knowing what she was getting herself into. And yet suddenly, she realized with a sinking feeling, that it was not going to be enough.

Her heart wanted everything.

CHAPTER TWELVE

AYAAN WALKED INTO the suite assigned to him in the Siyaadi palace and stared at Zohra's sleeping form in his bed. Familiar desire and something else—a fierce longing—wound through him at the sight of her.

He should have known he would find her here waiting for him, refusing to let him avoid her, refusing to let him hide.

But then, he still couldn't get used to the fact that she shared her body, her mind, her life with him willingly.

Restlessness that was becoming second skin scoured through him. He paced the perimeter of the bed, his gaze constantly straying toward her.

He had been fighting the cloud of awareness that had been coming at him for the week he had spent here in Siyaad. But this time, he was not enough to stop it, he could not hide from what he became, what he was changing into because of Zohra.

Because of the woman who deserved the best any man could give.

He had understood, been fascinated by, Zohra's strength from the moment she had stormed into his suite and stood by him through his nightmare. But this past week she had become something truly magnificent, she had become a princess. And she hadn't needed anything from him.

She had been a lioness when defending her brother and sister from the manipulative clutches of her extended family, a clever, quick study in her understanding of the immediate state affairs that needed to be organized, a formidable opponent to anyone who had dared question her role in King Salim's affairs.

She had been a sight to behold when she had addressed the nation of Siyaad after her father's funeral.

Ayaan had finally understood why King Salim had pushed for this marriage. He had thought marriage to the crown prince of Dahaar would achieve for Zohra her rightful place in the world, remove the stigma of her birth.

And yet, in just a week, Zohra had proved how wrong her father had been. She had needed neither the weight of the Dahaaran crown behind her nor Ayaan's support— either as her husband, or even as a man who could validate her place in Siyaad, in the way their archaic culture dictated.

But the primitive instinct in him that had somehow been nurtured by his madness of five years had risen to the forefront again. Why else would he feel things an educated man, a man supposed to lead his nation on a path of progress should be ashamed to even think?

Her strength in the week following her father's death, her confidence in taking on any number of challenges without quaking, the conviction of her own beliefs—Ayaan had been alternately amazed and weighed down by it, the worst of his fears crystallizing into undeniable truth.

Resentment was an acrid taste in his mouth, followed by utter shame at the level he could sink to.

He was a worse man than he had ever thought that he had indulged, even if for a few seconds, the idea of Zohra being a weak woman, of Zohra needing his help, of Zohra leaning on him for strength.

Even growing up with archaic customs that elevated a man while downplaying a woman's role, he still had never looked down on a woman. How could he when he had grown up surrounded by his mother's quiet strength, Amira's cutting wit and incredible confidence?

And yet Zohra's strength had only brought out his inadequacy, the bone-deep chill that said she deserved so much more than he gave her.

After knowing the resentment and sheer indifference Zohra had faced for so long, after hearing the echo of that pain still reverberating in her words, this conflicting whiplash of his own emotions, the wave of his intense desire and the crest of his self-condemnations, this was what he had to give her?

Caught up in his own personal pain, he had retreated from her, instead of standing by her. Of course, he had been by her side for all the public ceremonies and state functions. But he had not once inquired after her as a husband, had not offered a moment's comfort as a lover, had not even extended the minimum courtesy of meeting her eyes.

Because he had been terrified that she would see the truth in his eyes.

And still she came to his bed, she still sought him out, she still wanted to share his nightmares.

She would forever try to save him while he would damn her.

Even that realization was not enough to keep him from her. The greed inside him to be near her, to touch her, to feel her hunger for him, had no bounds or rules.

Pulling the long tunic he wore over his head, he climbed onto the bed. He turned on the bedside lamp, and lay on his side, content to watch her. He pushed strands of her silky hair back from her face.

Leaning on his elbow, he rubbed the pads of his thumb over her mouth, the familiar ache in him building with the velocity of an approaching storm. He sucked in a deep breath.

He had accepted long ago that it was always going to be like this with her. Nothing had changed. The pleasure he found with her was intense, binding him to her. He rode the wave at night, until nothing but self-loathing remained during the cold light of the day.

This fierce princess had become his salvation and his purgatory.

Zohra came awake the instant she felt Ayaan's hard body thrashing next to her. Sleep melted away as his soft whimper traveled over her skin. She turned the bedside lamp on just as his arm shot out. She held it hard between her hands, the chill of his skin a shock to her. Hot tears rose to her eyes. Turning to face him, she held his shoulders, the drumbeat of her heart thudding in her ears.

Sweat beaded on his forehead, the tendons in his neck stretched out tight.

Just as she had done that night so many weeks ago, she whispered to him, ran her hand over his forehead and tried to calm him. She had no idea how much time had passed before the tremors that racked through him stilled, the shadows of pain on his face retreated. She brought his palm to her cheek, forcing back her tears. She kissed every ridge and mound on his palm, breathing his name into it, feeling every inch of his pain as if it was her own.

His gaze fell open and landed on her.

And she braced herself for his wrath. He looked at her, his expression inscrutable, his mouth a straight line that gave no hint of what he was thinking.

But he didn't speak. Instead he pulled her down to him,

his breathing still uneven from the physical energy he spent during the nightmare. When he pulled her into the embrace of his body, Zohra melted into it, joy bursting out from her heart. It was more than enough for her that he understood that she wanted to be here, that he didn't question her right.

She tucked herself in as close as she could get to him. His arm was a heavy weight over her waist, their breaths slowly finding a matching rhythm. Her bones felt like they were molten, a strange mixture of lethargy and well-being turning her blood sluggish.

His hand moved over her arm, over the indent at her waist, up and down, again and again. His face was buried in her hair, his breath fanned over her nape. Just the fact that he was holding on to her, drawing comfort and strength from her presence filled her with an incredible, quiet joy. It was an intimacy that tugged at the deepest part of her, that burrowed itself into her skin.

She needed no words from him, she wanted no declaration of love. She only wanted to be by his side for the rest of their lives, to be there whether or not he needed her, to learn from him what honor and duty truly meant, to help her brother become an honorable, strong man like him.

She pulled the hand that rested under her torso and buried her face in it, tried to choke back the tears that somehow had gained a foothold in her tonight.

She had no idea how long they stayed like that and she didn't care. His breathing evened out, his touch offering comfort to her. She was scared to even breathe for the fear of fracturing the moment, for the fear of reality intruding on it.

Until suddenly his touch changed, his breathing raced.

His palm still moved over her bare arm, over the dip of her waist covered by her silk pajamas. But now his fingers pressed into her, demanded her skin react to his touch, remember every line and ridge of his palm. His other hand became seeking as it stole under her arm. The moment his long fingers covered her breast, Zohra moaned and shamelessly arched into it.

She had no idea how he disposed of her pajamas, or when he pulled her top over her head. Except suddenly, his body was a furnace of desire behind her. His chest rasped against her back, his erection a delicious, heavy weight against her buttocks. His leg covered hers, moved over hers creating a delicious friction that she wanted to feel everywhere.

His fingers pulled at her nipple, and she sank deeper into the mindless pleasure he incited. His erection lengthened and hardened against her. The image of the rigid length tucked against her bottom sent sparks of pleasure exploding over her skin. As sweat beaded her forehead, a relentless ache built in her groin and she moaned.

"Zohra?"

A whisper, a question, a command—her name on his lips reverberated around her.

Did he doubt her compliance? Did he not realize yet that her mind, her body, her soul—they were all his to command?

"Ayaan," she replied simply, knowing that he would understand.

Languorous heat uncurled inside her at the friction of his palm over her inner thighs.

The other hand continued playing havoc with her nipple, pulling, tugging, bursts of sensation arrowed down straight to her sex.

She moved restlessly, needing his touch at her core, her skin too frayed to contain her. He instantly understood. His fingers delved through her curls, opened her for his touch and stroked the quivering bundle of nerves. And then he thrust two fingers inside her.

Her release was so close that Zohra closed her eyes, clasped his wrist tight as if afraid he would stop. He kissed her temple as though understanding her need, whispered scandalous words that drove her another inch closer. Her entire body was poised over the edge, desperate to soar, when he rubbed his thumb over her clitoris.

Again and again, with a sure rhythm that toppled her over the edge. Her orgasm exploded inside her, turning her body into a million sparkling lights.

Her muscles were still quaking with the force of her release, her lungs struggling to catch a breath when he said, "Lift your leg, Princess."

His tone was nothing but raw command. Not that Zohra wouldn't have done anything he asked of her. She lifted her leg and he entered her.

This time, there was nothing but carnal intent, nothing but desperate desire in the way he thrust inside her.

The force of his passion, the wild abandon with which he took her, did not scare her. She followed where he went, trusted him with her body, splintered again when he wrenched another orgasm from her oversensitized body but underneath his desperate caresses, underneath his uncontrollable hunger, Zohra could sense a black cloud building.

His body convulsed behind her, his climax going on and on but even his hard kiss on her mouth couldn't shake her fear that something was terribly wrong.

Her muscles were weightless, her skin clammy with sweat. She made no sound as he picked her up and walked to the attached bath. Something was coming, she knew it in her bones, something wrong. But this time, she had no courage to face it head-on, no energy to fight. So she stayed silent, let him wash her in the huge sunken tub.

When he tugged her to him in the tub, she went willingly. When he pulled her onto him until she was straddling him, she hid her face in his shoulder. When he kissed her softly, slowly, as though she was the most precious thing in the world, she melted. When he suckled at her breast in deep, long pulls, she thought she would burst out of her skin. When he ran his hands all over her body, masterful, exacting, inciting, she gave in to the pleasure riding her again. When he buried his face in her neck and thrust upward into her, she let the tears fall.

He didn't ask her why there were tears and she didn't tell him. She didn't ask him what drove him tonight and he didn't tell her.

His hunger for her was insatiable, his every touch, stroke and kiss increasingly desperate and less controlled. And Zohra's need for him was no less powerful. Every caress, every sensuous assault of his mouth, of his fingers, she took everything with a relish and returned it back.

At some point, *when* she knew not, her mind simply shut down and Zohra sighed in bliss. She only wanted to feel right then. He carried her back to the bed. She thought he would find his own bed. But he didn't leave her.

He pulled the quilt to cover them both, kissed her temple and Zohra gave into sleep.

This time when Zohra woke, she was instantly aware of the exquisite soreness between her thighs. Every muscle quaked, her blood ran sluggish in her veins. She looked toward the huge windows and realized dawn was almost there. At some point during the night, she had lost count of how many times she had woken up to Ayaan kissing her, stroking her, tasting her, loving her, as if he couldn't talk himself off the ledge, as if his thirst for her knew no beginning, no end.

And every time, she had been right there with him, shocked at how much pleasure her body was capable of feeling, of how addictive and exhilarating it could be every single time.

Realizing that the bed was empty, she stood on shaking legs. Even tugging her thick hair back and binding it into a ponytail taxed her arms.

She slowly pulled on her pajamas and a silk robe, sensing his presence close.

She found him in the sitting area. His hands on his thighs, his upper body slanted forward, his very posture radiated tension.

For a few minutes, Zohra hung back by the sheer curtains that fluttered in the predawn breeze.

It had been two weeks since she had left him in the desert encampment for Siyaad, two weeks in which she had mourned her father's death, helped Saira and Wasim deal with their own grief, and somehow also found the strength to step in front of her family and face them down. Even though Ayaan had arrived only a few days after her, and had been present at all the important events.

He had not, however, said even a word to her since his arrival.

Lost in her own grief, she hadn't minded. His silent presence had been enough for her. She had borrowed strength from it, knowing that he would catch her if she fell, even if he didn't put it in so many words.

She had been so grateful for his presence that she hadn't realized when something began to fester between them, something she couldn't identify even as she racked her brain. She could feel the connection they had found slipping from her fingers like sand, could feel him retreating but had no way to stop him.

So she had come to his bed, despite the fact that he had

forbidden her to be near him at night. And just hours ago, she had been ecstatic that he had slept next to her, hadn't asked her to leave.

But now, the same silence stretched taut around them, deepening the chasm between them, dragging him further and further away from her. She must have made a sound because he looked up. And sprang to his feet as if she were an explosive that could detonate any second.

Even in the meager light of the table lamp, she could see the dark color that rode those sharp cheekbones. "Zohra, you are…I…I lost all control."

Heat pumped to her own cheeks now. She struggled to hide the questions that shot at her from all sides. "I am fine." She shoved the fear that was clawing at her and smiled. "Everything you did, I wanted, Ayaan. Was I not vocal enough?"

His gaze burned brighter, hotter, the sharp angles of his face reflecting the tightly reined in emotion within him. "*Ya Allah,* I behaved like an animal. I…"

She covered the distance between them and practically fell into his arms. She couldn't bear it if he became a stranger again. "I am definitely sore, though."

His curse should have turned the air blue. His hands stayed on her shoulders, his entire body stilling in that way of his.

She kept her arms around his waist, and found comfort in the fact that he hadn't pushed her away.

"I am sorry you didn't get a chance to speak to him, Zohra," he said, piercing the heavy silence, his embrace a safe haven of warmth.

The storm of regrets and grief she had kept at bay while shouldering her responsibilities for the first time in her life broke through at the tender concern in his words. He held her as she cried softly, for her, for her father and for her mother, for everything she had lost through sheer pig-headedness.

She met his gaze, and smiled through the tears. "He left me a sheaf of letters that told me everything I wanted to know."

"Letters?"

She nodded. The truth had hurt, but it had also freed something inside her. "Letters from my mother to him, even after he had left us for Siyaad. With pictures of me. Letters she wrote him until the day she died."

Ayaan frowned. "Are you saying she knew?"

Zohra nodded again, seeing the same confusion she had felt mirrored in his gaze. "She knew everything about him. She knew that there might come a day when he would have to leave her for Siyaad, to do his duty. And he did, just as they had known he would have to. He left us but they kept in touch. They argued, even in the letters. He asked to see me, and she refused, again and again. Said she didn't want me to pay the price for the happiness she found with him, didn't want me to be caught between them. I guess I was never supposed to know that he was alive. Except something happened that neither of them foresaw. She died. And...."

Her throat seized as Zohra realized once again what it must have cost her father to learn of her mother's death and to bring her to Siyaad.

"I can't believe King Salim could have been so selfish, so reckless," Ayaan said, pulling her out of the pit of regrets.

Zohra frowned at the anger that simmered in his words. "I was angry when I read those letters, angry that neither of them told me the truth. Even after I was old enough to understand. But not anymore.

"They took a chance on love, Ayaan, they grabbed their

happiness while they could, decided whatever short time they had was still worth it. Knowing that they had loved each other, knowing that my father had never deceived her, knowing that he loved me enough to bring me here—" Tears ran over her cheeks again. "—it fills me with joy. How can I hold the fact that they loved each other so much that they risked such unhappiness for the rest of their lives against them?"

Her body stilled as Zohra waited for his answer. Her heart pounded as his silence gave the answer his lips didn't, and one she didn't want to hear at that.

She ran her fingers over his jaw, over his cheekbones, traced the scar above his eye, as fear held a visceral grip inside her chest.

"You told me your mother never really smiled again after he was gone, that she wouldn't even look at another man. That to the day she died, something in her was forever broken while he…he moved on with his life. Had a wife and started a family."

Looking up at him, Zohra braced herself, knowing that the very ground that she was standing on was going to be pulled out from under her. "Weren't you the one who understood the need to sacrifice your own child in the name of duty? My father did his duty but he also let himself love. He took a chance and found happiness even if it was for a limited time."

"He damned the rest of her life in the name of love. He made you pay the price."

"They both paid the price, Ayaan. It was a decision they made together." She straightened herself, striving to fight the cold chill that was seeping into her. Every word felt like an effort. "You don't agree with me?"

"No. But what I think does not matter, does it, Zohra? What matters is what you think." His voice roughened in texture, as though he had to catch a breath to continue. His fingers caressed her face, desperate, fierce. "What matters is, apparently, you are exactly like your mother. You have the brightest spirit, the biggest heart I have ever seen."

His words should have elevated her to a higher place, should have filled her with happiness, but they didn't. The hard edge to his words only heightened her sense of something being very wrong.

"But I am not like King Salim. I will not damn you to a life filled with unhappiness."

His words knocked the breath out of her, tilted the very axis of her life. And Zohra forced herself to ask the question that was quietly gouging a hole inside her. "What are you saying?"

Ayaan fisted his hands behind him.

She took another step in. "Answer my question."

"You deserve a better man, Zohra. You need a man who will love you, who will cherish you, not use you at night and then expose you to his insecurities the next day." It was the hardest words he had ever spoken. "I do nothing but take from you, I have nothing to give you."

Her anger pulsed between them, just as sharp as the desire that suffused the very air around them. "Why do you not see what you have already given me? Honor, respect. You are my strength, Ayaan. I wasted thirteen years of a good life, lived it as if in a cloud, lived it with so much anger and hurt inside. I see you and I am ashamed of myself. I see your strength, your sense of duty, your honor, and I think this is what I want to be. You have not complained once at what you suffered. You push yourself every day to rise above yourself, physically and mentally.

"I do not care that you froze in a fight when you were barely a man. You have proven yourself to the world a thousand times over. Do these not count toward something?"

"It is not my strength or my lucidity that I doubt anymore, Zohra," he said, once again struck aghast by how perceptive she was. He had pushed himself in so many ways with a raging need to prove his worth to himself. He had pushed himself to the breaking point, to the last frayed edge of his mental and physical strength.

And he had emerged the victor but the hollowness in his gut had not faded. In the face of Zohra's strength, in the face of his own guilt and recriminations, they counted to nothing. "It is what I cannot give you, *ya habibati*."

"You have no right to call me that."

"The sounds you make when you come are still ringing inside my ears. I will call you whatever I please."

She shook from head to toe, her fury a palpable thing. Her mouth curved into a sneer even as tears shone in her eyes. "Not if you break the vows you made to me, not if you banish me from your life. You will not touch me, you will not even utter my name on your lips, Ayaan. Are you ready for that?"

He could not bear to see her like this—hurting, breaking. "I do this for you, Zohra."

"Don't you dare tell yourself that. You do this for yourself, to satisfy the guilt beneath which you have decided to live. So what happens now?"

"You will stay in Siyaad for an indefinite time. Your family needs you, Siyaad needs you. No one will wonder at your absence in Dahaar. And when the right time comes, I will let it be known that we have separated, that it is I who is lacking as a husband."

Her tears drew paths over her cheeks, bitter anger turning those beautiful brown eyes into molten rocks. "And the power to make that decision lies solely with you?"

"Something inside me is broken, Zohra. All I want to do is to lose myself in you, hear my name fall from your lips, again and again, but..." He gripped his nape, struggling to find the right words. "It will always be followed by this emptiness inside, by this self-loathing that I cannot fight. Before long, you will be stuck in that vicious cycle too and I will corrupt everything that is good and beautiful about you."

Her arms around her waist, she swayed where she stood, the pain in her eyes shredding him. But he had to hold fast for her sake.

"You have conquered so many obstacles, overcome so much for so long to become the man you are today, to become the prince that Dahaar needs. Can you not fight this last demon, Ayaan, for the woman who loves you with every breath in her body, with every—"

Ayaan placed a finger across her lips, but not before her words blasted through him with the force of an explosion. His stomach tightened, his throat seized up. Time seemed to have frozen at that minute. Looking into her beautiful, giving eyes, he wondered how he could have been so blind.

The love and acceptance there knuckled him in the gut.

She pulled his hand off her mouth, her slender shoulders trembling. "Truth, remember? The truth doesn't change because we don't want to hear it. I am in love with you. And whatever you face, we will fight—"

"I cannot fight it, Zohra. It is stronger than me."

She pummeled his chest, her slender shoulders shaking with the force of her anger. "It is not that you cannot fight it, Ayaan. It is that you don't want to fight it."

"You think I want to forever be a man haunted by his past—"

"Yes, you do." Her words echoed around them, bounced

off the walls, ringing with her belief. "You have judged yourself, found yourself guilty and you accepted this as your punishment. Not once in the time I have known you have you railed against it, not once have you resented it. You resent the fact that you cannot beat it but not the why of it. You cannot take a chance on us because God forbid you find happiness while your siblings are dead, right?

"And if you cannot see that, if you want to live the rest of your life stifled under that guilt, then you *are* right. You are not capable of loving me, nor do you deserve my love."

Ayaan stood there, unmoving, unblinking as Zohra wiped her tears and left his suite, left his life. The same way as she had entered it—shifting the very foundation of everything he stood on.

She was in love with him.

That incredibly amazing, wonderfully strong woman loved him. Even with his heart splintering inside him, Ayaan felt the high of her words in a dizzying whirl.

Of everything she had said, he knew one thing was for sure.

He was already in love with Zohra.

He was not surprised by the realization, or shocked. He simply, irrevocably, undeniably was. Maybe if he hadn't fallen in love with her, they could have had a life together. A life free of any emotional complications, a life free of passion, a life dictated by duty and mutual respect.

But it was the life-altering, heartbreaking love that flowed in his veins for her that made him question everything he was and he was not, that wished he was a better man for her.

He sank to the sofa behind him, his shaking knees refusing to hold him up. The scent of her was etched into him, it surrounded him, intensifying the hollow ache in his gut. He had thought he had known the worst in his life. But he had been wrong.

Nothing could be worse than the aching void in his gut. He would never look into Zohra's eyes, never see her laugh, never feel her touch again.

CHAPTER THIRTEEN

THE DEAFENING QUIET of the desert snarled inside Ayaan's mind, scratching its fingers up and down his spine. He forced himself to picture Zohra, laughing at him, challenging him, loving him. The fear didn't recede but the thought of Zohra diluted it enough for him to not fall back into its pit.

He could have left this matter to his security team but something he couldn't shake had lodged in his mind. Something about this man niggled at him.

It had taken Imran a month to unearth all the hidden sources of the recent terrorist intelligence and of course, it had been traced back to the same man who had fed them information the first two times.

Which meant he had intentionally covered his tracks. And Ayaan had instantly known something was wrong. It had taken his team another two weeks to find his whereabouts, two weeks of hell, in which Ayaan missed Zohra with an ache that had become a constant companion.

The whisper of harsh breathing, the sounds of footsteps, which he wouldn't have heard on the gravel road except for the fact that the man's stride was out of step, fell on his ears and Ayaan leaped from his crouching position behind the tent.

He couldn't have taken a breath before a blow came at

him, grazing his jaw. Shaking off the jolt of pain up his jaw, Ayaan returned a blow, and pushed the man to the ground. The man's leg shot out from under him, and Ayaan tackled him to the ground, his heart leaping into his throat.

Moonlight flickered over features that were as familiar as his own. A deathly chill fell over Ayaan as he collapsed to the desert floor, his muscles quivering with shock.

His throat choked with tears, his chest so tight that he thought he would explode. Shock waves paralyzed his mental processes as he stared at the man he had worshipped his entire life, the man he had held in higher regard than his father, the man who had taught Ayaan everything he knew.

The man who had fallen in front of him five years ago while Ayaan had froze, had stood there like a coward.

The desert wind howled around them as his heart pumped again. Surprise abated and a joy, unlike he had ever known flooded Ayaan.

His brother, the true prince of Dahaar, was alive.

Ayaan dismissed the security outside his office in the main palace wing, closed the door behind him and ran a hand over his eyes. His head pounded as if someone had hammered away at it relentlessly. He had been awake for forty-eight hours straight, and sometime yesterday, right when his mother had started crying as though her heart was breaking—again, a twitch had begun behind his left eye.

He knew that this was only the beginning of the hardest time of his life. And the fact that he had turned his back on the one woman who would have brought him solace, who would have understood his pain, who was the one shining point of his life, was an acrid taste on his tongue.

Since he had returned to Dahaar two days ago, the hours had seemed endless, each blending into the next, the things he had to take care of unending, until he thought he would break under the weight of it all.

He had kept Zohra's face at the forefront of his mind through it all, drew strength from the image of her warm smile, rooted himself in her belief that he could beat anything.

He had bent but he had not broken.

Now he was exhausted, both physically and mentally, and he ached to see her, to hold her, to share this fresh grief with her.

Ya Allah, he would give anything in that moment to hold her.

Pushing away from the door, he walked past the sitting area into his office beyond.

And as though he had conjured her out of his very imagination with sheer desperate craving, there was his wife, pacing the floor. Emotion knotted his throat, rooting him to the spot.

He must have said her name aloud because she was hurtling toward him before he could blink. She hugged him tight, then stepped back, her gaze hungrily sweeping over him.

"I heard the news. Is it…Is he…" She frowned. "How are you taking it? You look…exhausted."

Ayaan blinked, a host of emotions vying within him—the need to hold her tight against him was the strongest. He sucked in a deep breath, greedy for the scent of her.

Until she had spoken, he hadn't realized how good it was to be asked, to know that his state of mind mattered. Of course, it mattered to his parents too, but right now, they needed him more than he needed them.

She was dressed in stylishly cut gray trousers and a light blue silk blouse. The delicate arch of her neck, the strong pulse thudding there, the stubborn jut of her chin, the flare of her arrogant nose—he was starving for the sight of her. Shaking his head, he tried to focus on what had bothered him about her statement. "Only four people know that he is alive."

"Khaleef told me," she said, the concern in her voice fading back. "And before you bring down your wrath on him, remember this, Ayaan." Her voice broke on his name, but she continued, her chin tilted high. Pure steel filled her words. "I care about Dahaar, about the king and the queen. I have every right to this information."

Despite the journey to hell and back in the past two days, Ayaan smiled. And in that very moment, he saw what he had been too blind to realize until now. This beautiful, amazing woman was a gift he had been given and due to his cowardice he hadn't been able to accept it. "Are you done, *ya habibati?*"

"No. And you can't send me back to Siyaad either." Her words reverberated with a confidence that brooked no argument, but her tight fists at her sides gave her away. "I refuse to hide, refuse to lick my wounds in private as I have done for so long, refuse to let someone other than me decide my fate, decide what I deserve and what I don't.

"Whether you want me or not, I am your wife. I have a right to live in Dahaara, a right to learn everything I need to be the Dahaaran queen, a right to your parents' love. I have earned my place, Ayaan. And if you can't bear the sight of me, then it is on your head. But you try to send me back and I will show you what a Siyaadi princess is truly made of."

It was the most magnificent sight he had ever beheld. His heart pounded in his chest. He moved closer and ran his fingers over the pulse beating frantically at her neck. "Adding to my nightmares, Zohra?"

The resolve in her brown eyes melted, giving way to the

cutting pain she hid. It punched him in the gut. "If that is how you see me, then so be it. But I have never wanted to be the cause for your—"

"Shh…I meant it would be a torture to be near you and to not touch you, to not hold you." He breathed into her hair. Tugging her toward him, he held her at her waist, loosely, striving for control over himself. "All I feel is joy when you are near, pure, freeing, like I have never felt before. How can you think you bring pain?"

"I will kill you myself if you leave me again, Ayaan." Fighting words, but Ayaan heard the pain in them.

"Shh…." he said, and ran his palm over her back, up and down, more to soothe himself than her. She was so fragile in his grip, and yet inside where it mattered this woman he had had the good fortune to marry, this woman he had had the temerity to fall in love with, had a core of steel and a heart as big as the desert.

And he would spend the rest of his life loving her as she deserved to be loved.

He touched his forehead to hers, his heart lodged in his throat. "You brought light into my life. If not for you…" He shook as the grief he'd held at bay since the minute he had laid eyes on his brother burst through him. Tears he couldn't stem, tears that needed to be shed, wet his cheeks.

Her slender arms tightened around him, her body a cocoon of warmth. And everything she gave him was a precious gift. "Ayaan?"

"I have seen what it means to be truly broken, Zohra."

Her heart crawling into her throat, Zohra clasped Ayaan's chin and tugged it up. Fear beat a tattoo beneath her skin. Even in the most painful moments, even when he had been drowning in his nightmares, she had never heard such stark desolation in his words. "Whatever it is, Ayaan, we will beat it together."

"You have already saved me, *ya habibati*. I was just too stubborn, too blind to see it. But he…there is nothing inside him, Zohra."

A ghost of a shiver passed over her at his words. "Your brother?"

"If eyes were windows to the soul, then there is no soul left in him." He tugged her hard against him, his arms steel vises that could snap her in two. Rising on tiptoes, Zohra held on, letting him take what he wanted from her.

"I was so afraid, Ayaan. Khaleef said he was in bad shape. And my heart sank. I thought seeing him like that would mean—"

"That guilt would claw through me once again? It does. It hurts so much to see him like this. But the worst is knowing that for God knows how long he has been aware of his identity and he has been in hiding. If I hadn't followed up on that hunch, we would have never known he was alive. He doesn't want to be here. And even in the state he is in, it took both Khaleef and me to force him to come with us. And my mother, *Ya Allah*—"

"How is she?"

Ayaan smiled and kissed her again, intense sadness still clouding his eyes. "He refuses to see her or my father, said he will put a bullet through his head if I bring her to him."

Shock waving through her, Zohra frowned. "You think he would?"

"Whether he is bluffing or not, he knows I won't risk calling him on it. He said he wants to be free of this family, he wants nothing to do with any of us. If I became mad, he…he has devolved into pure emptiness. Maybe my madness protected me from the worst."

Anger fired those words and Zohra stared at Ayaan. His family, his duty, his country—they had always come first with him.

"For the first time in my life, I wish I could walk away from all this, steal you away, give you a life free of my demons, a life free of duty... All I want is to prove my love to you but all I see is more pain, more sorrow ahead. If you leave me...if you walk away, that is what I will become, too. And I don't want to, Zohra.

"I want to live with you, I want to laugh with you, I want to snatch any happiness I find with you. If you don't leave tonight, there is no turning back, *ya habibati*. I will never ever let you go again, not even if you beg me."

He clasped her cheeks, his long fingers greedy in the way they moved over her. His gaze shone with everything Zohra wanted to see in it when he looked at her—his pain, his honor and his love. It was all she ever wanted. "I am in love with you, Zohra. You were right. I let guilt pollute everything I felt for you, everything I found with you. But no more, *ya habibati*. You and I and our happiness together, I will allow nothing to mar it. Will you still have me, Zohra, knowing what lies ahead for us?"

Zohra kissed him, melting into his embrace, joy flooding every inch of her. His hunger matched hers, as his mouth moved over her lips as if he would never get enough. "There was no turning back for me from the moment you kissed me, the moment you came to my defense, the moment you said my honor was your honor. I will always love you, Ayaan."

She tucked her face into his shoulder, she clutched his shirt in her fingers, striving to fight the depth of emotion that overpowered her. The love she felt for him had already been fierce, but now that he had accepted it, now that he had admitted what she and their happiness meant to him, it flew through her with an incredible force.

She would allow no one to add to his burden, not even

the brother who meant everything to Ayaan. She would allow no one to steal even an ounce of happiness from him.

"You can't give up on him, can you? I am sure he knows that, too. And whatever you have to do for him, for Dahaar, I will be right by your side."

His fingers moved over her cheeks, his gaze glittered with a happiness that stole her breath. "I am never going to stop loving you, Zohra, will never forget what you brought into my life."

"And what you brought into mine, Ayaan. Never forget that either."

He nodded, kissed her again and picked her up. "There is one problem, *ya habibati*. I still don't think you should be sleeping beside me at night. I don't want to ever wake up and learn that I hurt you even a little. I couldn't bear it."

Breathing through the happiness that constricted her chest, Zohra nuzzled into his neck. "I have the best idea about how to take care of that, Ayaan."

Gold fire lit up his eyes.

"How about we cuff you every night before you sleep? That way, I won't get hurt and you are…"

Ayaan laughed, the naughty glint in his wife's eyes sending a thrill running through him. The guilt, the pain, they would all forever be a part of him, but as long as he had Zohra by his side, he would tackle them. Because he also had a taste of utter joy. "Your wish is my command, Princess."

* * * * *

A sneaky peek at next month…

MODERN™

POWER, PASSION AND IRRESISTIBLE TEMPTATION

My wish list for next month's titles…

In stores from 18th April 2014:

❏ The Only Woman to Defy Him – Carol Marinelli
❏ Gambling with the Crown – Lynn Raye Harris
❏ One Night to Risk it All – Maisey Yates
❏ The Truth About De Campo – Jennifer Hayward

In stores from 2nd May 2014:

❏ Secrets of a Ruthless Tycoon – Cathy Williams
❏ The Forbidden Touch of Sanguardo – Julia James
❏ A Clash with Cannavaro – Elizabeth Power
❏ The Santana Heir – Elizabeth Lane

Available at WHSmith, Tesco, Asda, Eason, Amazon and Apple

Just can't wait?

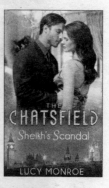

Join the Mills & Boon Book Club

Want to read more **Modern™** books?
We're offering you **2 more** absolutely **FREE!**

We'll also treat you to these fabulous extras:

- 🌹 **Exclusive offers and much more!**

- 🌹 **FREE home delivery**

- 🌹 **FREE books and gifts with our special rewards scheme**

Get your free books now!

visit www.millsandboon.co.uk/bookclub
or call Customer Relations on 020 8288 2888

Discover more romance at

www.millsandboon.co.uk

- ❤ WIN great prizes in our exclusive competitions
- ❤ BUY new titles before they hit the shops
- ❤ BROWSE new books and REVIEW your favourites
- ❤ SAVE on new books with the Mills & Boon® Bookclub™
- ❤ DISCOVER new authors

PLUS, to chat about your favourite reads, get the latest news and find special offers:

- 📘 Find us on facebook.com/millsandboon
- 🐦 Follow us on twitter.com/millsandboonuk
- ❤ Sign up to our newsletter at millsandboon.co.uk

M&B_WEB